THE SHARP THEORY

JAY CHAUHAN

ISBN: 9798838368737

To Ruth.

My wife, my life, and my Inspiration.

And to my children, Nina, Kiran and Aneil, to who I wanted to show that anything is possible at any stage of life. Including writing a book.

A special thanks to Laura Tellwright,
for her help with the initial edits of this book.

About the Author

Jay is a Doctor of Philosophy and is currently the director of AmbaCare Solutions CIC, linking health, social care and housing. He is a highly skilled professional, with extensive senior manage-ment experience within the statutory, public and voluntary sectors. As CEO of a Housing Group and an Urban Development Organisation, he developed general and special needs housing and social care schemes across the West Midlands. Jay worked in the NHS across both the acute and primary care settings for 14 years. He was involved in developing and supporting a number of acute and community-based initiatives, for example, an Integrated Intermediate Care Unit, community-based COPD & Integrated Diabetes Education & Research Centre (IDEA Centre) and Dementia training programmes.

When Jay is not devoting his time to his family and the local community, he is concentrating on Dementia research as he is also the founder of Dementia Diversity, an initiative of AmbaCare Solutions. He is currently involved in developing several health & wellbeing and dementia programmes.

In Jay's debut fiction novel, *The Sharpe Theory,* he uses his strong background in the health sector to combine the subjects of dementia awareness with the popular genre of crime and thriller.

1

Madison Sharpe was lying sprawled on her back, with only the sad sky above to bear witness to her plight. She couldn't quite bring herself to sit up just yet. Instead, she found herself glaring up, teary-eyed at the cumulonimbus clouds above as if they were to blame for all her problems. She heard Emily snorting as she pounded off into the distance. Madison had been warned not to ride her without a helmet and now she was furious at herself. Her head throbbed. She knew she would end up with a bump on the side of her forehead, at the very least. She urged herself to take relief in the fact that she, at least, wasn't concussed because that certainly wouldn't have been very pleasant.

Something had spooked Emily, the horse, and she had taken off at a gallop. Had they been out in the open fields it wouldn't have mattered, but the horse had bolted for the woods - too far into it for Madison's liking. And as Madison struggled to keep her balance atop her leaping mount, a low-hanging branch had scooped her straight out of the saddle.

It was lucky the ground was soft from the autumn rains that month or she may have ended up cracking a bone or two. The fall had been comical, and she was glad that no one was around to witness it.

"Ow!" A pain ate at her hip as she lightly sat herself up. Emily had trotted off to a nearby grove and was curiously sniffing around the bushes. Her solid back muscles flexed as her roan muzzle drove into the thicket of leaves and wild flowers, all of her panic long forgotten.

Emily, a high-strung thoroughbred, was only six years old and a trained school horse. According to Karl, she had the build and versatility of a racehorse, but thoroughbreds rarely ever raced and therefore grooming her to be one would be costly and futile. But her arrogant temperament and competitive need to overtake her opponents was perfectly suited to the racetracks. For this reason, she was often rented out by novice racers. But an untrained horse her size was hard to control, especially when she was startled.

Madison had heard it too; the loud guttural feminine scream that could have only come from an urban fox. The ranch was privately owned, as were the woods surrounding it. It grew denser from where she sat on the cold grass-laden earth amidst the thinly dispersed oak trees surrounding her. The owner only allowed the horses to be taken out to the tracks, the polo fields or just along the thin trail beyond it into the sparsely wooded region surrounding the clear areas. Further beyond lay the denser part of the woods where deer, foxes and a rumoured bear frequented.

"There are no bears on this side of the country!" she had told Karl, the only son of the owner of Brayton Riding School. He had informed her about the supposed bear he'd seen along the dirt road that led up to his ranch.

"You wouldn't be saying that if you saw one digging through *your* trash! Believe me, and I know what I saw. Trekking trips with my good old Uncle Howard taught me a thing or two about bears, and that *definitely* was a bear raiding my wheelie bins. Three in the damn morning!" he had said, grimacing at the thought. "Straight out of a nightmare. Couldn't sleep a wink that entire week!"

Karl Brayton and his wife, May, had moved to London a few decades ago. Karl's parents had long since abandoned their life in this isolated part of the New Forest District in favour of a more zealous one in the US. However, in his adulthood, Karl had longed to revisit his roots and made the decision to return so he could convert their family house into a ranch; a very successful one at that.

Madison pulled herself to her feet, brushed off the bits of leaves and soil from her faded jeans and made an attempt to close in on the brown mare, only for the beast to trot further away.

"Come on now, that's too far in," Madison moaned to the animal, who neighed irritably at her patronising tone and continued to move further along.

Madison considered following Emily but thought better of it after a moment. Although the sun was hidden amongst the clouds, it was coming down so she would have to leave soon if she wanted to make it back home before dark. She couldn't bring herself to bother about a disagreeable horse this late in the day, especially when it looked like it would rain any second.

Massaging the growing bump on her forehead she was about to turn away and walk back, deciding that she'd let Karl handle the beast, when she heard the gentle sound of hooves closing in. Madison held out her palm, letting Emily approach it, and as she huffed a wet breath against it, Madison smiled. "That's right, good girl." Having sensed her approval, the horse playfully pushed her cheek against Madison's open palm and nickered. "Cute… But I still would have left you!"

The ride back was uneventful. Madison gazed at the vast stretches of densely vegetated lands; at least what was visible in the thin fog that hung over the tall trees. The lush greenery and fresh air always carried an unadulterated rich aroma of wildflowers and wet earth. Madison understood why Karl had chosen to come back - she would have done the same.

Situated in the outskirts of Lyndhurst, Hampshire, the wooded property was named St. Elwyn, after a 16th-century resident, Charles Elwyn Nye. The 400 or so acres of soft hills and fertile land harboured within it the largest riding school within a 100-mile radius from the City of Westminster. A well-frequented campsite for scouts and several popular Airbnb spots could also be found there. Additionally, it was home to several species of wildlife.

After a prolonged legal altercation between the Brayton's and The Forestry Commission, Karl was allowed to retain the land. Therefore, St. Elwyn remained the only privately owned wooded property in the area. But the sound of hooves and heavy bodies against the polo field, the occasional loud crack of the mallet hitting the ball, followed by the resounding yells from players as they stalked the ball on their mounts, made the area far more spirited than those adjoining it.

But that day, the characteristic chaotic din of St. Elwyn was absent. It stood sombre and still. The grassed fields were too wet and slippery for a safe game, the weather too grim and precarious. The quiet was unnerving to Madison's aggrieved and tired mind.

The fox hadn't cried again, and the awful stillness in the air hung heavy around them. The sound of hooves hitting wet soil haunted her and she wondered if the cry they had heard was actually from a person. She knew that was not the case, but she couldn't help but shudder at the thought. It would need an ungodly amount of pain inflicted on a person for them to make that kind of sound. The kind of agony that stretched bare the very vocal cords of a human being.

One time she had witnessed an opioid addict impale himself on the spear of a twenty-foot-tall copper statue of the Greek God Ares after falling from a roof in an attempt to flee the raid that Madison had spent months organising. That particular drug bust had been one of the very first cases that she was allowed to lead. Although, the sight of the man slowly getting ripped in half as he slid down the smooth, beautifully carved shaft of the giant spear, painting its surface a claret red, had slowly ebbed from her memory in the many years following the incident - the man's hellish screams of agony, slowly settling into a low moan as all life left him, paired with the soft sound of tearing muscles and cracking bones, remained evergreen in her mind. That was the first time she had wholeheartedly wanted to quit her job. She didn't, and she had lived to regret that decision.

Understandably, she wouldn't want to be anywhere near that kind of agony now because that incident was only the tip of the iceberg to the years of brutalities and death that she would experience in her career—all of it leading up to a case that would end up ruining her life.

And with that pleasant thought came running her paranoia. Her heartbeat quickened. Even the slightest rustle of leaves made her double-take. Her eyes wildly sought out an invisible pursuer that she knew her mind had made up, but still, in her occupation, one couldn't be too sure. Her hands, drained of blood and ice-cold, gripped painfully at the reins as she urged the horse to pick up speed. Only when she reached the clearing did she loosen her grip.

To worsen matters, the fog had developed thicker over the open fields and made it nearly impossible for her to spot the light brown structure of the barn, or most of the racetrack for that matter, while the adjoining stables and structures were almost entirely enshrouded.

She tugged at the rope and carefully steered the horse in the direction of the barn. She considered dismounting but she couldn't risk Emily running off or into a fence when the visibility was low, especially when the paved ground beneath them was slick from the fog. Still keeping a watchful eye out for any unusual movement, she managed to find her way.

Just when Madison's mind had convinced her that her imaginary pursuer had lost her, a soft, almost rueful melody filled the silent air around her. She frowned - her fingers tightening around Emily's reins.

Emily nickered in protest over the sound of a distant piano. A sense of panic filled Madison. Was her mind playing tricks on her?

"I'll see you again. Whenever spring breaks through again."

Noël Coward's voice sang hauntingly in the quiet space. His high tenor lingered within the white desolation around her. Her hand automatically flew to the holster wrapped around her waist where her phone was strapped in.

Her face warmed with embarrassment, as did her hands which came as a relief against the prickly, sweat-covered rope that her fingers still gripped at.

She muttered a curse as she pulled out her phone. Noël Coward's voice now louder and clearer.

"Learning scales will never seem so sweet again."

That's right. Somehow she had set Noel Coward's, 'I'll see you again' as her ringtone in a late-night drunken stupor whilst enjoying his songs on the local radio. During those late hours nothing seemed quite as beautiful as Coward's voice in her mind. Her restive soul wanted him to soothe her every time a toilsome phonecall demanded her attention. That night, she had set the phone back to silent; the resonating vibrations of her phone against her wooden nightstand were loud enough to wake her up. She had only set it back to general that very morning, weary of the fact that she might miss an important call on her day off, completely forgetting about her new ringtone.

Cutting Noël off mid-verse, she accepted the call. It was from Allison, the smart-mouthed PhD student she had taken on to manage the phones and keep her paperwork in order.

Allison was exceptionally good at her job. She was intelligent and tidy; to the point of obsession. She had a filthy sense of humour and a chirpy personality to match - the qualities Madison's small detective agency needed with the unsettling variety of tawdry jobs it sometimes took on.

But the girl had no sense of time. It was 5 p.m. on a Saturday and the office was supposed to be long closed by then.

"I hope this is urgent, Allison," Madison panted out into the phone.

"Oh, sounds like I caught you right in the middle of... Sorry!"

"You've got a disgusting mind."

"Right, that Fincher woman's been on the phone again. She's annoyed because you haven't called her back."

"What does she want?"

"She says it's private. I'll text you her number."

Madison sighed as the line went dead.

The first rumble of the clouds rolled through the sky as she sped towards the open doors to the stables. She found Phil's muscular form bent over in one of the stalls, grooming one of the older horses. His sleeves rolled up to his elbows as he held up the equine's leg on a stand and carefully knifed the ends of its hoof. Phil was a six-foot-eight giant with a burly build and a shaven head, but his loud and risible demeanour did wonders to neutralise any intimidation his build otherwise offered. He wore a grin as he looked up to welcome her approach.

"Back at it again, I see," he called. Returning to his work he asked, "Is it drizzling out there?"

"No. Not yet," Madison replied as she brought Emily in and waited for Phil to take the reins from her. "But there's a really thick fog. Best not let anyone else ride out."

"Yeah. Karl called a while back asking me to close up," Phil nodded absently at his work as he finished up and freed the staggering horse's leg from the stand. "Was about to go and look for you. The fog wasn't that thick this morning, guess it's been getting colder."

As he stood up and saw Madison his smile turned to a snigger. "Must have taken quite a fall there, Miss Anne Shirley. Told you to wear your helmet, didn't I?" He walked up to her, brushing off his large hands against his trousers. He sucked in a breath through his teeth as he observed the modest-size bump protruding from her head. "That's quite a goose egg! Better put ice on that before it swells and pops."

She rolled her eyes handing him the reins. "I'll live."

"I'm sure you will," he smiled as he walked Emily into one of the empty stalls and locked her in. "C'mon, let's get you an ice pack."

She gave him a quizzical look.

"I promise you I won't pull anything funny," he said with his hands raised defensively.

She pursed her lips in hesitation but complied sheepishly.

2

Madison followed Phil to the small office adjoining the stables. She had been in there many times before, as well as inside the family cottage just beyond it. She had actually solved a case for the Braytons a few years back and had become something of a family friend to them. She loved their farm, and the woods surrounding it. Even taking up riding lessons at their school as an excuse to spend more time there after she gave her resignation at the bureau.

"Oh, and that's the third strike, Miss Anne Shirley. We catch you without a helmet again and we'll be forced to revoke your membership," he offered playfully as he unlocked the office and let her in.

"I'm not sure Karl is ready to get rid of me just yet."

Phil merely grinned.

Phil had taken to calling her Anne Shirley since the very beginning of her membership at the riding school a few years back. He had caught her riding the same equine without her helmet out in the vast clearing. The wind had swept her ginger curls across her face and the name had slipped out of his mouth almost involuntarily; loud enough for her to catch it in the blowing wind. The name hadn't surprised her back then, what did take her back was the fact that a rugged stable boy like Phil knew his classics.

"Take a seat," he said as he wandered over to the mini fridge standing next to the vintage office table.

Pulling the small office chair from against the table she sat down. The room was a tastefully decorated wooden shed, big enough to fit, at most, three people comfortably. The brown brick walls, covered with pictures of horses and people that she didn't recognize, smelt of new paint.

"There are not many people out today," she remarked attempting to run her fingers through her knotted hair.

"There's no one out. We aren't allowing people inside the forest anymore, not until late December at least. And no one showed up today because of, well, the fog. But apparently that wasn't enough to hinder your arrival, Miss Shirley."

Madison snorted. "I don't think I'll be able to come by much this month so I figured I'd show my face one last time."

"New case?"

"Mhm."

"You know," Phil said, leaning back against the edge of the office table, facing her. "Karl and May were relieved when you quit your job at the bureau. They were convinced that kind of job isn't suited to you, or anyone sane for that matter."

"Not this again!" she fell back against the chair.

"So, when you went sauntering back to it a year later, they were understandably upset. And I can see why now."

"And why is that?" she challenged. Phil shook his head. "No, tell me!"

"Do you ever look at yourself in the mirror?" he spat, raising his bushy brows as if he were the one offended by her lifestyle. "Ever really observe the transformation you've gone through these past few years?"

She narrowed her eyes at him, observing the misplaced anger, the superficial worry on the man's face for a quiet minute. She realised she couldn't fight him. He believed he had the right to be angry at her because he genuinely thought he cared for her.

She decided she didn't feel any anger towards the man. "I'm old enough to take care of myself. May and Karl respect me enough to keep their distance, despite their disapproval of how I've become. And I appreciate that." A smile slipped onto her face. "But I'm fine. I'm trying to be fine… for real this time," she said, trying to sound as convincing as she could.

But it was Phil's turn to narrow his eyes sceptically at her. The sympathy was evident on his face, but there was something else seeping through the apparent pity and anger… repugnance? But he was quick to hide it.

"Eat your meals, Sharpe," he scolded. His tone shifted to one of warm hostility. Phil raised his hands defensively. "As much as you hate coming down here every other week, it's the only way they know you're still alive."

"I don't hate coming down here." And she didn't. Her weekly trips to the ranch were the few things she still enjoyed. What she did hate was the unending enquiries about her lifestyle.

Phil shook his head. "Karl dreads the thought that one day you won't show up, and he'll get to learn about your untimely demise, possibly from alcohol poisoning, on the TV, or worse – from one of your ex-colleagues at the bureau. And I know he'll kill them. He can't stand bobbies, especially the ones bearing news of your death. I sincerely hope you know that."

Madison snorted at that. "I'm fine. Even if I do die, they won't show it on TV, so the latter is more likely."

"You've worked on some high-profile cases. Even made some

TV appearances. I'm sure some conspiracy theorist will join some non-existent dots together and claim the government killed you off."

"What goes on inside that head of yours? I just - I can't seem to keep up with you," she sighed. "Also, it's been almost three years since I left. They would've killed me off by now if they really wanted to. Why wait this long?"

"I don't know. Maybe for the right moment."

"Huh. Could be," she said thoughtfully.

"No, *seriously*. Karl is worried sick. You don't call them so they never know what you're up to. You're nothing less of a daughter to them, you know. And they don't have kids, so would it hurt to be a bit more considerate of their feelings?"

Phil had been working at the riding school for almost ten years. He was a local and this was, at first, a summer job but he kept it, even after he finished school. He himself was nothing less of a son to the Braytons, having known them since he was a toddler. His parents were often away, like the Braytons, on various business trips or vacations, and so Phil was the one who looked after things in St. Elwyn in their absence.

"I'll call them more often." She had no intention to, but the least she could do was offer Phil a verbal acknowledgement, however much of a lie that was.

"Thank you," he said, raising his brows as he turned away again.

"Why aren't you allowing people inside the woods?"

"Well, the weather's a big pain, but mostly because it's open season," he said, pulling out a bag of ice then letting the door to the fridge fall shut. He took an ice pack out of a desk drawer, poured a few ice cubes into it and tied the opening before testing the pack against his own wrist.

"People hunt in Elwyn?"

"No, not exactly *in* Elwyn." He handed the pack to her and walked over to the window. Leaning against the sill Phil watched as Madison put the pack to her forehead. "Mainly in the woods surrounding it. Since there's no visible divide between Karl's property and the woods around it, except for a century-old wooden fence, most of it is broken or claimed by the vines. Some people tend to wander over to our side of the land and shoot up animals. Can't have those scouts or camping hippies around when we have stray bullets to worry about."

Madison nodded. The throbbing in her head had dimmed to a mere ache as she worked the ice pack around her head.

"I swear none of those fat cretins can shoot straight. I'm surprised they haven't shot up each other yet," Phil grimaced. "Would do the world some good if they did."

She couldn't help but chuckle at that. "What do you have against them?"

"I just don't get the existence of those damned hunting associations. Animals are getting killed off as it is. Putting a label on it and doing it for fun is just...wrong."

"Well, they're entitled to their way of thought, as long as they're not doing anything illegal. What do they hunt?"

"Big game, small game. Grey partridges, muntjacs, hares. Anything the commission allows."

"I saw this Red deer with vitiligo once, by the tree lines. And I still don't understand why it didn't scurry off after seeing me. Somehow, it was not afraid of me. It had these roundish white patches around its body and head, like a cow. It was kind of beautiful. A few months after that encounter, I went out for dinner at the local diner and there, right next to the bulletin board listing the menus was the deer's head; all stuffed and polished, mounted up on a wooden board for all to see." Phil grimaced as he recalled the sight of the head of that once fearless deer.

"People like to boast. Even if it's done at the expense of life or innocence, it gives us a sense of validation that, in turn, gives our life meaning. That's human nature," she figured.

"Does that mean you need validation too?" Phil asked with an upturned brow.

"No. I think I've outgrown that need for now. And how does that leave me?"

"Disappointed and angered by everything and everyone in this world."

"Exactly!" she chirped, feeling the squish of the melting ice inside the pack against her fingers.

"What a way to live."

"You get used to it after a while. I bet the fog foiled your hunting clubs' plans."

"Yeah. I hope so. The fog usually comes later in the year, though," he offered absently, gazing at the whiteness outside before turning to her again. "Think you can make it back home like this? Maybe you should wait until it clears."

"I don't think the streets will be too bad."

"Still."

"I'll be fine."

"C'mon. Stay. I'll go get that vintage liquor Karl's been saving up, and we could drown our sorrows until the fog clears."

"Stop."

"It'll be fine."

"I've got work tomorrow. Anyway, Karl will go mad if he finds out you raided his wine cabinets for me." She stood up, offering him a smile. "This worked though," she said, gesturing to the purple ice pack before setting it down onto the office table.

He didn't reply. Instead, he returned his gaze to the window.
"I'll get going then." She shot up and made for the door.
"Drive safely, Miss Shirley."

3

The fog was clearing up but the clouds looked angry. The Brayton Riding School parking space was only a minute walk away from the office shed, but it seemed longer than usual with the eerie quietness of her surroundings.

As she was climbing into the driver seat of her rustic Ford Bronco she caught sight of a figure standing by the tree line that led into the woods, just beyond the reach of her eyes. She blinked against the low visibility of the foggy air, but when she opened them again, she saw no one.

She didn't think much of it and got into her car.

Madison rolled her shoulders gently as she sped through the highway. Thankfully, the fog had cleared up completely a few miles ahead of Elwyn, and there weren't many cars out either. What little sunlight the storm clouds overhead allowed made the miles of densely forested areas appear somehow grimmer than how they appeared in complete darkness. The fog that still hung over the distant trees made for an almost dreamlike, outlandish scene. It all seemed extremely morose, yet Madison found herself revelling at the sight.

She wondered absently if she should look at properties closer to this part of Lyndhurst.

The drive back was smooth, and the only time she got stuck in traffic was when she got to Chinatown, which was understandable.

Waiting for the traffic to clear up, she glanced out the window at the busy takeout place on the side of the road. A neon sign that read 'Bibimbap' in big red glowing letters hung over its entrance, slightly tilting to its right. The place was a familiar haunt among her colleagues since Harry's PI firm stood right behind it, in a relatively dim and inactive corner of the neighbourhood. She couldn't see it from her car, but she knew it was there. The vast grey building wedged between a theatre and a small Chinese thrift shop. At first, it had given off a rather grim appearance, compared to the buildings around it, but with time, and the enlivening efforts of Chinese lanterns adorning the streets, the firm had started to fit in.

She had grown quite fond of the enclave during her time spent there. The cultural richness, the ever-flowing crowds of people through the streets, the life it exuded even as late as two in the morning. It teemed with a sense of vibrancy like no other place she had ever been to. It was, after all, one of the liveliest parts of London. The wild mixture of exotic scents from the food stalls and restaurants, challenged by the lingering stench of sewage and rotting fish, felt somewhat homely to her.

Soho lay just around the corner. Equally active and inviting, its narrow bustling streets gave way to pastel-coloured buildings as well as a myriad of theatres and shops. And just along the stretches of attached buildings of all sizes stood Madison's archaic double storey apartment. The buildings were old and residential, mostly rented out by students and temporary residents looking for cheap housing in the affluent area. Therefore, getting too close with your neighbours in Soho was out of the question.

Every building came with its own tiny backyard, which no one ever tended to because no one ever stayed long enough. But Madison had no excuse for the deplorable condition of hers. She'd been living in the same apartment since the day she started working for Harry; a little over two years ago. She had shared the apartment with a student for a while, who kept to herself, and it was during her brief stay that she had tended to the yard.

By the time she unlocked her apartment door the rain had started to come down hard. The pitter-patter of rain against the roof was somewhat comforting. After wriggling out of her wet riding clothes and taking a quick shower, Madison reached for an unopened bottle of 2010 Gevrey Chambertin. Phone in hand, she flopped herself on the living room couch and searched for Elizabeth Fincher's number.

Elizabeth Fincher picked up on the second ring.

"Miss Sharpe! This must be your private line. I've been trying to reach you all day." Elizabeth spoke firmly, with a characteristic lisp and a condescending tone.

"I've had a few prior engagements. This week was a long-anticipated time off for me, which I believe I told you already the last time we spoke," Madison added as she balanced the phone between her ear and shoulder while reaching for the bottle on the table.

"Oh! You did, didn't you? I must be getting old," she chirped pleasantly.

Elizabeth Fincher was a thirty-year-old, la-di-dah colleen who had her antlers caught in the branches of aristocratic trouble. A once naïve, soft-spoken sweetheart, now hardened into a rock by the day-to-day turmoil of the unforgiving, top drawer world of her spouse. At least according to Madison's sources. Her husband, who was the current subject of her self-denying revulsion, was a successful entrepreneur. Charles Fincher was a man of fifty-five and a bachelor until recently. He and Elizabeth tied the knot only a year and a half ago, although they had known each other a long time.

The youngest of six siblings, Charles Fincher was a fellow with a very mild temperament but was an ingenious and cunning marauder in his field of business, up until he was diagnosed with moderate dementia. This sudden condition of his coincided almost too suspiciously with the untimely disappearance of thirty million dollars from his bank account! Notified to Elizabeth by her trusty accountant, only a week after Charles' diagnosis, that their funds were running suspiciously thin.

Things were heated as it was for the young Elizabeth. Yet the flames of her turmoil were further fanned by the arrival of a stranger; an American businessman named Simon Kane. Allegedly, her husband owed him a colossal sum of twenty million dollars. And now, in the absence of Charles, he was hounding Elizabeth for the money.

"I suppose you heard back from Kane?" Madison inquired as she poured the wine into a glass.

"I did," Elizabeth spat. "The man has taken to threatening me now."

"Have you tried contacting the bank?" Madison asked before taking a generous swig of the sweet liquid.

"My consultant called the Bank of Nova Scotia. They're doing their best to track down the transaction. They're convinced that the money was in the account in early October. A withdrawal was made somewhere between late September and early October that went unrecorded. So, there's our lead. I also asked them if they would release a client's money in the event of an illness, such as Charles' and they were quite helpful." Madison could hear Elizabeth's voice soften at the mention of her husband's illness, but she continued. "With an attorney, medical certificates and an international lawyer, they said it was certainly possible. The only catch being that even if I did want to pay the absurd amount Kane's been demanding of us… I simply couldn't. Not without us losing the house and just about everything to our name."

"Has Kane provided any documents attesting to the loan?"

"No. None. He tells me that Charles wanted the payment to be made entirely in cash, that he didn't want a paper trail leading to him for this."

"That's a major red flag, Mrs Fincher. Is there a *chance* Kane could be lying about this?"

"You see, um… there's a thing. I…uh, I really can't have you disclose this. It's important to me that you understand that."

Madison considered the hesitance in her voice for a moment. "Our agency's terms of non-disclosure bind me from ever doing that, Mrs Fincher," she assured.

Madison only received a prolonged pause to that.

"See," Elizabeth finally said, "we've known Kane for a while now and still, I would be ever ready to call Kane's bluff, especially on this particular matter, but he tells me that Charles handed him a painting as collateral." Elizabeth hesitated, "A-Are you familiar with the works of Claude Monet?"

Madison sat up. "The French impressionist? You're telling me your husband put up a Monet painting as collateral?"

"Shocking. Isn't it?"

"But that alone should cost considerably more than what Charles owes him."

"Yes. About 30 million more! It does have quite a value to it, doesn't it? Which is why me being bitter about its loss is completely justified." Elizabeth's voice shook with rage. "I'm really not allowed to speak much about it, but it was a rather unexpected wedding gift from Charles' late uncle, Sir. Michael Rawlins. I'm told it was his family heirloom, but since Sir. Rawlins didn't leave behind an heir most of his property went either to charity or was passed down to his many nieces and nephews.

"The painting is one of Monet's unnamed works. And no one, aside from a few family members and a selective team from the ECCO, who have signed a strict non-disclosure agreement, knows of its existence. This brings me to why I believe Kane isn't, in fact, bluffing about Charles owing him money. You see, Kane described the painting in vivid detail. There's no way he could've done that without having seen it at least a few times."

"Where was the painting kept? At your house?"

"No. It was kept inside an underground vault with our other assets in our Boston property. We intended to keep its existence a secret since its hefty worth would certainly make it subject to unwanted attention, and Sir. Rawlins arranged for the same – for it to be stored away and cared for in private."

"I take it Charles didn't consult you when he put up the painting as collateral?"

"No!" Elizabeth shrieked. "If he had we would not be having this conversation!"

Madison gave Elizabeth a moment to calm down - the sound of her enraged panting filled the other end of the line.

"I'm just rechecking the facts, in case I miss something," Madison offered in a calm voice.

"Sorry," Elizabeth muttered as she steadied her breathing. "I understand. It's just – it's been a lot. With his illness and everything going on. I just feel very *lost.*"

"Anyone in your position would feel the same," Madison assured. "Did you check with your staff at the Boston property?"

"I did," Elizabeth said, clearing her throat. "They told me they received direct orders from Charles for the painting to be packed up and brought out."

"Where to?"

"No idea. Probably to Kane's office," she added bitterly. "I'm the wife, Miss Sharpe. They won't give that kind of information to me!"

Elizabeth cleared her throat again and began in a steadier tone, "My husband, however, claims he did no such thing. Sweet Mary Joseph! Forget taking a loan from Kane, my husband doesn't even remember the man."

"What do *you* think about that? Is there a possibility he might be lying to you?"

"See, the painting has a rather steadfast value to Charles, like his uncle before him. It is treated like an object of worship rather than a measly asset. Which is why learning that *he* had given it away had been all the more distressing to me. But, in his line of work nothing holds more value than money.

"Kane has been a trusted financier to Charles as he was to him. They went to college together and had been doing business with one another for a long time. They trust each other. So I'm guessing unofficial loans, such as this one, had been fairly common between the two.

"But now I'm the one picking up the pieces. I'm the one getting harassed for the money. And I have none to spare because most of it is gone! If we don't find the money soon, we will lose the painting. For good."

The peculiar pause between them urged Madison to put her thoughts into words.

"One of the two is definitely lying."

"Simon doesn't have reason to lie. He cannot sell the painting legally since the whole ordeal was unofficial and undocumented. So he has no proof to claim that the painting is his to sell legally. But he can get value for it elsewhere, and I have no doubt he knows where. His goodwill towards our family is the only thing keeping him from doing it, but his patience is wearing thin.

"But then again, you don't do that. And you don't just give away that kind of money with a simple verbal promise, not even to your own mother. So maybe he *is* lying," Elizabeth quizzed herself. "My consultant offered another plausible explanation as well."

When Elizabeth said nothing else Madison urged her to go on, "And what is that?"

"That Charles could be faking his illness. Perhaps he simply ran out of money. Or maybe his illness is somehow related to the missing millions. Which is why I need you to get on to it as soon as possible, by any means necessary. I think that's our best bet at getting anywhere from here," Elizabeth stated sharply.

"I will try my best. I do have one more question though. Do you have any clue why Charles would need that kind of money from him, off the record at that?"

"No Idea. I try to keep as far away from his wayward businesses as possible. Well, until now."

Madison considered that for a moment with an amused smile. She placed the now-empty glass on the centre table and sat back against the couch. "I think I'd like to pay you a visit. A chance to speak with your husband, if possible."

"Of course," Elizabeth accepted. "I'll mail you the address first thing tomorrow."

The melody of a recent pop song drifted in from outside, over the sound of the beating rain. University students rented most houses in the area with deplorable music tastes and raging addictions to video games. Blasting EDMs and house parties were quite frequent in the area - most residents were already used to the noise.

Madison sang along to the song as she busied herself in the kitchen preparing dinner.

"What's for dinner, honey?" she mumbled to herself between the words of the song.

"Pot pie!" she answered, eyeing the stale piece of pie rotating inside the oven.

The couple living in the apartment next to hers were engaged in a severe verbal altercation. Their voices carried out over the rain and through the slightly-open window of Madison's kitchen. Neither paid any heed to the infantile colic of their two-month-old baby.

It's none of my business. She reminded herself.

By the sound of it, they had probably left the window open in the second-floor nursery. Which, she guessed, was probably right next to the baby's cot.

She tried to sing over the sound of their screams and her own thoughts, reminding herself yet again that it was *none of her business.*

"Goddammit!"

Madison grabbed her phone from the living room and dialled the number she had saved as 'side-neighbour2'.

"Hey, Jamie, it's Madison from next door..."

The sound of shuffling feet and cussing came from somewhere in the distance. "Oh, hey Madison, it's really not a great time."

"Yeah, I'll be quick. I noticed a spark near your weatherhead. I think you should have Grayson check it for any fires."

"Really? Oh God - Grayson!" she yelled for her husband. "I'll call you back, Madison."

As soon as Jamie hung up, Madison walked over to the kitchen window overlooking her muddy, overgrown yard. She peered up at the second-storey window of Jamie's apartment and caught sight of a panicked Grayson, shuffling around in the nursery. She could hear Grayson yelling at Jamie about the open window over the shrieks of their baby.

It took a while for them to get the baby to calm down.

At least there won't be any more fights tonight, she thought as she caught a whiff of her burning pie. She clicked her tongue, realising she had forgotten to set the timer on *again*.

Dumping the charred pie in the trash, she snacked on a few crackers, downed a beer and passed out cold on her messy bed.

4

Sir. Conan Doyle had described Esher as the 'pretty Surrey village,' and in all honesty, it does still live up to that title. Even to this day. It offers a rather delightful mix of rural tranquility with just the right urban noise. It accommodates, within its verdant wraps, a combination of lavish estates as well as adorable little cottages. All would be nice in this town, if only it wasn't for the snobbish gits residing in it.

Madison's work had sent her this way on several different occasions. Each time she'd not had great experiences with the residents. She wouldn't have much problem with babied snobs - who would hire workers at the drop of a hat for even the slightest inconveniences - if it weren't for her already dwindling hope for humanity that urged her to vilify every passing soul that had the misfortune to cross her path.

At least they paid well.

That morning she found the trash bags, left outside the previous night, slashed open and spilling over with pools of accumulated rainwater in front of her apartment.

"It's the stray dogs," Jamie called out to her from her window, regarding her with a friendly smile. "They're all over the place poking around in other people's business."

Despite her frustration, she had calmly brought out a broom

and swept away the pieces of spoilt lettuce, that she didn't recall having that week, and left for work without another word to spare to the woman.

But the whole situation had taken a toll on her mood. And she still found herself tensing with annoyance as she leaned back against the satiny white love seat spread out in the Finchers' massive living room. She crossed her legs and tapped lightly on the glass of cold water that she had been offered on her arrival.

"Mrs Fincher will be with you in a moment," the assistant, probably in his early twenties, dressed sharply in what Allison would call a 'geek chic' attire, declared smartly before taking his leave.

Madison had never underestimated or questioned the extent of the Finchers' opulence. It seemed all the more impressive to her, seeing it firsthand. Although she made sure that none of the awe showed in her face.

Her own apartment seemed box-like and pathetic in comparison.

She'd never actually been one for big spaces. All the more since living by herself. Something about them being too quiet and echoey bothered her.

Obviously, much space was too destructive for an idle mind for any amount of time, and being left in the grand room all by her lonesome wasn't quite helping her case either. She tried to resist her fleeting thoughts; willed herself to focus on the task at hand. She was so tired. The drive to Esher had taken over an hour and the micro nap she had taken in the cab on her way to the Fincher house only contributed further to her languor.

She stifled a yawn and resisted the urge to take a sip from the glass she held. One thing she didn't like to do was eat or drink something that she hadn't made or served herself.

Allison had continually joked that this unnatural paranoia of hers was far-fetched, impolite, and would unsettle anyone in their line of work. Especially as feigning trust was a pivotal necessity. Madison had rightfully found herself acknowledging it as so, but she couldn't risk it. Her raging, obsessive-compulsive disorder wouldn't let her risk it.

After checking no one was coming, she leaned forward and poured the cold liquid into the pot that held a giant bonsai plant, atop a mahogany centre table. She placed the empty glass down and with her thumb casually wiped off the droplets that had sprayed on the table.

Digging the heels of her palms against her closed eyes Madison willed herself to wake up and focus. She leaned back against the couch again and exhaled.

One second she was staring up at the high ceiling chandelier, and the next she was blinking against a familiar scent drifting through the air around her.

The scent of Irish soda bread.

With the hair on her nape rising, her mind registered the scent of buttermilk. She only had moments to look up at the man rushing towards her. Dread hit her like a bucket of cold water when she realised she wouldn't be able to react in time, just as the butt of the pistol he held up connected to her face.

"Ugh." She pushed herself up from where she was settled on the couch. Violent tremors ran through her hands as she blinked against the darkness behind her eyes.

Jesus! Sleeping at a job, especially this soon after a week-long downtime was a new low, even for her.

The long gulps of breath she took didn't do much to subdue the tremors. Elizabeth Fincher picked that very moment to walk into the room.

"Oh! About time you showed up," Elizabeth's voice echoed through the walls as she strode towards Madison. The clack of her heels obnoxiously loud in the empty room.

Madison pushed her shaking palms against her lap as she sat up. Shoving them underneath the hem of her jacket, she hoped Elizabeth wouldn't notice them.

Thankfully, Elizabeth Fincher had other things on her mind. Her brows were furrowed with unease as she offered the open file. She took a final glance before closing it and placing it on the centre table. Taking her place on the couch opposite Madison, she reached an expectant hand out to her; oblivious to Madison's internal panic. "Pleased to meet you, Miss Sharpe," she smiled formally, clearly indicating that she was ready to get down to business.

Madison couldn't help the edges of her lips twist at the forced formality, but she let the smile show as she slipped her own shaky palm against Elizabeth's manicured one and tried her best to shake it firmly.

Elizabeth Fincher was a beautiful woman. Clad in a black pantsuit, she sported a tight high bun that enhanced her already sharp features. Her elegant red lipstick stood out spectacularly against her tanned skin. Even the minimal jewellery she wore screamed opulence. Mrs Fincher dressed to leave an impression, and that was certainly achieved.

"Well, I have heard a lot of great things about Harry's PI firm. He tells me you are one of his best," Elizabeth offered.

"That's news to me." It wasn't, really. She had the highest clearance rates among all of her colleagues, and that was no news to anyone at her firm. "That last time we spoke, he clearly told me that I was too wayward and careless to do well in this field."

Harry Booth, an ex-RAF veteran and the person who owned the PI firm Madison worked at, was a close friend of her fathers. Which often gave the man a sense of fatherly authority over her. She was honestly getting sick of everyone in her life trying to play family with her, especially when her *own* family couldn't care less about her.

Elizabeth chuckled at that. "He recommended you to me, the very instance I told him I needed this to be done with the utmost discretion. He seemed pretty confident about your skills, and I think I'll take his word for it. People of his age and credentials are usually very accurate about their perusal of people."

"Indeed. Let's say most of the cases we deal with require us to be tactful. Although knowing *why* does help us determine the situation better."

"Very well then. It's nothing out of the usual, really. We just don't want this situation to be blown out of proportion. Charles' family is... well, conservative, and they might not react very well to this. Some might even see this as an opportunity to take advantage of Charles. He's a precious man. We do not and will not have him harmed in any way."

Madison nodded. "I understand. I would, however, like to go over a few more things again regarding Mr Fincher before I get the chance to meet him," Madison expressed as she leaned back against the couch.

"Of course," Elizabeth answered, crossing her long legs and leaning back in her seat. "Go on."

"Would you mind if I record this conversation?" Madison asked.

"Depends. Who else will hear it?"

"Just me. For future reference only," Madison assured.

"No, then I do not," Elizabeth said with a curt nod.

With that, Madison reached into the pocket of her blazer and pulled out a voice recorder, placed it on the table between them and switched it on.

"Well then, Mrs Fincher, would you please reiterate your husband's condition to me," Madison said, leaning forward. "Please specify names and the dates if you may."

"My husband, Charles Fincher," Elizabeth started uneasily, "was diagnosed with Dementia on the sixth of November by his doctor. He had been showing signs of moderate cognitive decline as early as January. He started forgetting a few trivial things at first, like a misplaced cup or losing his reading glasses, for instance, but we didn't think much of it. It was only in September just gone that he woke up one morning looking for his late mother, Mrs Misha Fincher, who has been dead for quite some time now.

"When I tried to tell him that, he told me that I must've gone crazy because apparently, she was coming to visit him that very day, to take him away to Cheshire for the holidays."

"What did you tell him then?"

"The truth. That she has been dead for over twenty years."

"I suppose he didn't take that very well?"

"No. He didn't. Later that day he suffered a seizure. That was the first time things really started to get out of hand with him."

As the words left Elizabeth's mouth she raised her head and locked eyes with Madison. "I've seen him at his best, Miss Sharpe. He's a magnificent man," she spoke with great intensity. "And I always feel at my best when I have his attention. To see a man like him crumble right in front of my eyes is a sight you simply don't recover from. I couldn't do anything but gape at him. Luckily, Henry found us in time and got him to the hospital.

"The MRI and CT scans showed nothing, and it was only based on various memory tests and the abrupt changes in his behaviour that the doctor claimed it to be Dementia."

"What was your husband's reaction to the prognosis?"

"He took it surprisingly well. Like he had expected it," Elizabeth expressed, nodding to herself. "Which is odd. I mean, being diagnosed with something of this scale. Isn't it basically like a death sentence? But he just acknowledged it with a nod, very unlike him. That man, he rarely lets much out. Anyway, the next morning, when I brought him his prescribed medicines, he strongly insisted that he was fine. He didn't even remember going to a doctor. He claimed that *I* was the one who was ill for suggesting so."

"It makes you think he's lying?" Madison suggested.

"Oh, I know he's lying about something," Elizabeth confirmed irritably. "As I said, the diagnosis was done completely based on a memory test and his self-claimed cognitive impairment."

"How much does he remember?" Madison asked, rubbing her fingers against her temple as she felt the indications of an oncoming headache, probably from her lack of sleep.

"It's not all gone yet. He mostly acts like his usual self. He buries himself in his paintings all day and occasionally tends to his interns. Other times he forgets everything around him. He failed to recognise some of our own house staff, on more than one occasion. Sometimes he doesn't even recall what he did the day before."

Madison nodded at that. "That will be all. Thank you for your cooperation, Mrs Fincher." Madison turned the device off and dropped it back in her pocket. "Now, if you would be so kind to lead me to Mr Fincher, and then we can call it a day."

Elizabeth acknowledged with a smile as she gracefully rose

from her seat. "Given his fragile condition, I think it would be best if he remains unaware about your true profession. For now, at least."

"What should I tell him?"

"I don't know. Make something up," Elizabeth said with a careless flick of her hand.

5

Elizabeth led Madison to a pair of exceptionally large white French doors set ajar, that led out to a huge outdoor garden. A modest sized pergola stood at the center, facing what Madison guessed was the rustic dome of an old observatory. Close-cropped to moderately long grass covered the fields as if autumn didn't exist in this utopic estate of the Finchers.

It was under the restful shade of the white vine-covered pergola, surrounded by cans of paint and canvases of his own unfinished works, that Charles Fincher was settled comfortably on a wooden barstool.

With his back to them, he faced a brilliant incomplete portrait of a bearded man, in Victorian attire, balanced on a wooden easel. His left hand, which held a long brush, was smeared in paint and trembled lightly as he filled a portion of the portrait with an odd mixture of vibrant colours.

Charles was a large man. The pictures of him on the internet hardly did any justice to his actual size.

"Charles," Elizabeth called after her husband, who responded with a casual fling to his paintbrush. "I have someone here who would like to meet with you," Elizabeth said with an almost inconceivable edge to her voice.

"Oh, sweet Beth, we talked about this," he proffered casually, without looking back. "I don't need another shrink, now please, show him the way out before I get upset with you again."

Madison peered at her host, who was visibly cowering at her husband's assertion. But when she spoke again her voice held no traces of her physical tension. "She's not a psychiatrist, Charles. She's *my friend*, the one we talked about."

Madison raised her brows amusedly at her words.

Apparently, that was enough to catch Charles Fincher's attention, who swiveled half-way around in his barstool to regard Madison with a genial smile.

"Oh." He turned fully this time. "Apologies," he urged with a cheerful smile. "Henry! Fetch my guest a chair, would you?"

A man emerged from one of the numerous backrooms leading out to the garden holding up a white deck chair. He placed it a few feet from Charles who gestured for Madison to take the seat.

Madison complied with a smile mirroring his own.

"Well, I'll leave you to it then." With that Elizabeth turned and went back inside the house.

"Been getting cold, hasn't it, miss..." Charles trailed off, peering at her expectantly.

"Anne... Anne Murphy," she offered.

"Miss Anne," he said, his kindred smile still intact on his subtly wrinkled face. At first glance, one would say he didn't look his actual age, but as he smiled more, the slight wrinkles lining his mouth and eyes became more discernable. Madison noted that his clean-shaven face and his close-cropped hair contributed greatly to his youthful appearance. His loose-fitted maroon sweater did generously as well to dissemble his well-kept burly form underneath it. All in all, Mr Fincher presented a considerably plain front, considering his affluent status.

"It indeed has, Mr Fincher," she conferred, crossing her legs casually, leaning back into the chair.

"Please, call me Charles," he politely insisted as he returned his attention to the painting. "So, how do you know Beth?" he asked, dipping his brush on the flat palette resting on his lap.

"We went to Pembridge together." Madison gazed at the dull green flowerless shrubs on the painting. "But we only got in contact again recently."

"That must be nice, I'm not really in contact with any of my school buddies, sadly," he lamented. "What do you do, Anne?"

She raised her brows but replied without pause, "I'm currently studying for my master's degree in Humanities and working as an assistant to an author in my spare time."

"Oh, really?" he asked breezily as he worked on the painting. "What is he called? Perhaps I've read some of his work."

"Cameron Peters, one of his more notable works is 'The Hysterics of a Sound Mind', I believe," Madison answered without a hint of hesitation. "Although, I do have to admit he's a real grouch, aside from the sordid amount he pays me in the name of salary. But working with him keeps me somewhat solvent."

Cameron Peters was indeed a writer *and* Allison's uncle. He was a withdrawn fellow, with anger issues and a delightfully unsuspicious background that she could easily exploit during such times.

"Ahh Peters. I can't say I've heard of him," he admitted humorously. "Although, I do feel sorry about your predicament," he added with a dry chuckle.

"I must confess that... my mind has been all over the place lately, and I can't seem to recall why you wanted to meet me."

"Oh!" *Damn you Elizabeth.* "I'm writing a novel. My first one actually."

"Is that so? Well, what is it about?"

"I don't really know yet. For now, I'm just going about looking for muses and gathering meaty experiences from acquaintances and friends or whoever wishes to open up about themselves without taking offence. Ticked off quite a few strangers at bars in the process," she offered with a grin.

Charles laughed at that. A hearty, handsome laugh that softly shook the paint off his brush.

"Beth told me that you might be interested..."

"She did?" he asked, genuinely surprised. "Well rest assured, I'm not one to take offence too easily. And I don't really have much to do these days either. So, feel free to ask away to your heart's content."

From the orange rays of the sun that painted the grassed fields surrounding the pergola an unearthly golden, Madison guessed that it was past two in the afternoon. A good hour had gone by since her arrival at the Finchers' manor, and she was pleasantly taken aback by how quickly the time had passed.

There was no denying that Charles Fincher had a charming personality that delightfully fit with his equally attractive appearance. Although most of the conversation on her part were well-attributed lies, she still found herself enjoying it. He spoke about his life as a child and how he got himself through the struggles and prejudices that his opulent world had flung his way. He also talked about his career and when and how it took flight. He spoke of it all with a strange serene distance as if his own life was like a bittersweet soap opera, but all the same, he seemed glad to have lived and experienced it.

His bashful candour came as something of a surprise to Madison.

"My parents never separated on paper, but their marriage ended a long time ago. Mum moved to Cheshire; I couldn't move with her because my father wouldn't let me. But I did get to visit her every other summer and during the winter holidays."

"Were you close to her?" Madison asked.

"Yes. Every trip to her home in Cheshire was like an escape to me as a kid."

Madison smiled. "How old were you when she moved?"

"About eight. Too young to have your mother taken away and be able to come out of it emotionally unscathed." He chuckled drily as he considered the next colour in his palette. "It's safe to say I've had my own share of traumatic experiences."

Madison gazed thoughtfully at the man's rueful smile and felt her own fade.

"My uncle had a way with them, you know. He told me that bad experiences are like cigar smoke. You exhale it out hard enough, and your system is cleansed of it.

"He'd make me think of them, one bad incident at a time, telling me to breathe in as I recollected them and when it was finally time to breathe out, to release them all with the air I exhaled. And just like that those thoughts would cease to exist."

"Did it work?" Madison asked.

"Sure. If you're delusional enough," he said with a grin. "It worked for a while though. Or rather I forced myself to believe that it worked, but...," he shook his head, "you go on that way too long and it poisons you from the inside."

"Like cigar smoke?" Madison offered with a nod.

Charles chuckled. His lower lip catching the edge of his teeth.

"I suppose. His whole persona was based around conflict avoidance really, and baseless superstitions. He was obsessed with those too," Charles said after a moment. "That man, he could fool himself into oblivion if he really wanted to. But regardless, he was loved. He truly wanted to be happy in life, even in the face of despair."

"Sounds like you were quite fond of him," Madison commented.

"I still am."

She looked away to keep herself from staring at him - and his ridiculously fetching smile. She wondered if Charles had the same effect on others that he was currently having on her.

The silence that followed between the two was comfortable, peaceful even. Giving Madison enough time to brood.

There was no doubt that this uncle of his was Sir Michael Rawlins. Reputed art collector and philanthropist of the late 80s, and older twin brother to Charles' mother, Misha Rawlins. Their father, Doctor Amos Rawlins, did not have many articles to his name, or anything other than the ones stating his obvious occupation, under the numerous interviews from his elite children.

Charles hummed a tune that she thought sounded a lot like a Noël song and cringed at the recollection that followed.

She glanced at Charles. His lips were gently pressed together, as he forced the melody through his nostrils. He seemed at peace, the kind of peace you wouldn't want to ruin with intrusive questions. But she didn't have all day.

"How do you feel these days, Mr Fincher?" Madison asked finally.

The movement of the paintbrush on the canvas stopped, as did the melody, but Charles' expression remained unchanged.

And suddenly the tranquil silence between them grew progressively tenser and foreboding.

"I'd like to say I feel as healthy as a horse, but I would be lying," he said finally, as his hand resumed its work on the canvas. "By the sound of it you already know the gist of it."

"Beth slipped up about it earlier. But it really wasn't her fault. It was mine for prying," she added.

"I'm flattered that you find me appealing enough to pry, Miss Murphy. But Beth being Beth, she has a habit of blowing things out of proportion."

"Dementia is a serious-"

"I'm well aware of that," he insisted with a smile. He dipped his brush into the blob of bright teal, the only colour that sat untouched on his palette, and brought it up to stroke over the shaded brown of the man's beard. The teal stood out distastefully against the tinted brown. But Charles seemed to take no note of it as he continued to blend the colours together with his brush.

Madison wondered if that was all she would get, but then he spoke again.

"Oh, to have a clean slate again, wouldn't that be a wonderful gift?" He sighed turning to Madison. His gaze fondly observed the surprise in her face at the question.

But there was more to his gaze than just that. She saw awareness in his green eyes, the kind that wasn't supposed to be there. She felt a chill run down her spine. Charles certainly knew more than he let on. Madison wondered how easy it would be for him to find out who his wife had been in contact with these past few weeks.

But Charles wasn't admitting to anything so she wouldn't either.

Two can play that game, she thought to herself. "I'm sure Beth wants the best for you."

"That she does," he acknowledged, with a sincere smile that made his eyes scrunch up. "Poor her. Stuck with a meagre man like me," he lamented.

Henry emerged with a tray that held two cups of steaming coffee.

"I hope you like coffee," he stated as he reached to pick up a cup from the tray.

"I'm afraid I don't," she said with feigned guilt.

"Tea then?" Charles suggested.

She shook her head. "I'm fine," she told Henry, who offered her a quiet nod and took his leave.

She cleared her throat and said, "She is awfully worried. And that perhaps would be my other reason for coming down here today."

"To persuade me into answering her endless questions?" Amusement flashed in his face as he spared her a glance.

"She's in quite a bit of a quandary."

"She brought that upon herself."

"She tells me that, apparently, you owe someone a generous amount of money," Madison blurted, going in for the kill.

He hummed. "And what of it?"

"She told me that she doesn't really know what to make of that. Apparently, she hasn't found any paperwork relating to it."

"Ah, yes. She was never really that good with paperwork, that one. One of her more delightfully lovable traits I would say," Charles remarked fondly.

"She also tells me about someone called Simon Kane, who keeps calling, but she has no idea what he is talking about."

He chuckled light at that. "Sounds like Beth."

"I enjoyed my work quite a lot, but I think this break is well-deserved," he mused after a while, as he brought the porcelain mug to his lips.

"Do you think you would get back to it?" Madison asked.

"I don't know yet," he muttered, before taking a long sip.

"Well, do you have enough material for your book?" he inquired, setting the cup down on a small compact table that stood beside the easel.

"Not really. But I think this should do for now."

The disappointment she felt was palpable. Not only had the man sidestepped the question, again, despite his welcome, he had been dancing his way around the more relevant questions most of the evening. But the masterly ease with which he manipulated his words was something Madison had to give him credit for.

Charles Fincher had given her exactly what he had agreed to offer and had not spared a single extra detail.

She knew that she wasn't going to get any more out of the man that day and with a mental nod to herself, she looked down at her watch with a feigned sense of urgency.

"I think I've kept you long enough," she said apologetically as she pulled down the sleeve of her Jacket over her watch again. "I suppose I should take my leave now. Thank you for your time, Mr Fincher... Uh... Charles," she said rising from the chair.

"I must admit it was quite refreshing talking about myself. It gave me a chance to look back and see my life from a fresh perspective. I wouldn't want to sound too intense, but it made me feel quite... sane for a change. I almost feel that my life isn't as big a train wreck as I imagine it to be," he said with a smile.

"I'm glad that you feel that way."

"Although, the next time we meet I would like to hear more about *you*, Miss Murphy."

She let the smile slip away from her face at his words. She pursed her lips and simply nodded at his request.

As Madison strode away from the pergola she couldn't shake off the feeling that Charles' eyes were still on her, as if his unwavering gaze was burning into her very skin.

She found Elizabeth pacing nervously in the living room.

"It was lovely speaking to your husband."

"So… what do you think?" Elizabeth inquired.

"It's still too early to form an opinion," Madison asserted, walking towards the front door that led out. "I'll call you if I do have one later."

Elizabeth shot her an unreadable look and crossed the distance between them.

"I'm taking Charles out to a polo club this Thursday," she whispered. "He's in no state to ride but he's got friends who are, and they keep pestering me to get him out of the house. While we're out Henry can show you the way around," she said, flicking her chin at the man who stood in adept attention behind her. "I want you to search Charles' office."

Madison was taken aback by the wild request.

"It is off-limits to the rest of us and there's a good chance he might be hiding something in there. Henry might be able to get the lock for you. See if you can find anything on his computer or his cabinets that might help our case. I don't really know what he has in there, none of us have ever stepped foot inside that room. So, you make sure to check everything, okay?" Elizabeth said in a suppressed tone. "We will be leaving at ten in the morning. You will have two to three hours at best."

As she was ushered towards the front door Madison couldn't help herself from speaking, "He seems like a nice man."

"Indeed, he does! Until you get on his bad side."

"I might be able to learn more if I get to know *him* a little better."

Elizabeth glared at her with a soft tragic smile playing on her lips. "Go right ahead, if you wish to, darling. But let me warn you," she said, leaning in towards Madison, "he won't remember a thing about you."

***

Madison pushed the fiberglass gates that led into the agency building open with her shoulder. She was running on five cups of coffee and a twenty-minute nap and was ready to jump anyone who uttered a word about her scruffy appearance.

"Good morning, Miss Sharpe," Mary, the receptionist, called after her as she stepped inside the building. Madison forced a nod and clomped her way down to Allison's office.

It was only seven in the morning and Madison almost bawled at how zestful Allison appeared, settled on her seat with her head propped on her hand, peering up at Madison.

"Well, you look homicidal," Allison remarked with a smirk.

"Make another comment about my appearance and there'll be one!" Madison snapped, as she flopped down on one of the chairs facing Allison's desk.

"I need you to run a background check on this guy," Madison pulled out her phone, opened the screenshot that she had taken the night before and slid the device across the table towards Allison, who caught it with a finger and turned the screen towards herself.

"Simon Kane," Allison read aloud. "Is this from Facebook?" she glared at Allison, unimpressed.

"Yes. I need it by Thursday morning, tops."

"He's fifty, probably single," Allison muttered woefully as she stared at the balding man on the screen. "You could do better, honestly," she added with a grimace.

Choosing to ignore the remark, Madison instead explained, "He is the American businessman who's after Fincher's money."

"Hmm, interesting. He might have a wife, or two, then," Allison observed. "But that's completely fine," she insisted with an understanding nod.

Madison passed her a bored but dangerous smile and uttered a, "Mmh, so funny." Rising to her feet she collected her phone from the table.

"Are you done with the Peterson's case?" Allison asked just as Madison was about to leave. "They settled the payment during your time off."

Madison nodded. "It's like I said, the kid wasn't kidnapped. He ran away because his parents punished him for smoking grass at school. He was living at an older friend's house."

Allison raised her brows in surprise at the information. "Man, kids are really dumb these days, aren't they? Bet he met the older guy on one of those predatory gaming forums."

"Wait. That's classified. How'd you know that?"

Allison simply shrugged. "Heard the kid is suing you for invasion of privacy."

"I did track him down through his own bank card – kind of saw this one coming. I'm going down there right now to try and talk him out of it."

"Good luck with that," Allison sneered.

Madison decided to take the bus since she couldn't trust herself to drive with the dangerous levels of caffeine flowing through her veins. She tapped her boot against the pavement impatiently as she waited for the bus to arrive at the stop. She promised herself that as soon as she got home she'd take a pill or two and pass out cold until the next morning. With almost a week's worth of proper sleep to catch up on she felt particularly determined that day.

Her eyes wandered off to the busy footway across the street. A man stood by the water hydrant that faced the street. Most of his face was hidden behind a surgical face mask so she couldn't quite make out his features. Oddly, despite the cold, he was clad in a thin white t-shirt that seemed wet and clung to his skin.

When she realized he was observing her as she was him, she looked away.

Madison was relieved when a bus appeared moments later. Finding an empty seat by the window, she flopped down and heaved a sigh, letting herself untangle.

Leaning her head against the cold glass of the window her mind wandered off to the Finchers' case. She had been a private investigator for almost a decade, and cases like that were fairly common in her line of work. And she had thought that this case would be as boring and dull as most others she was usually assigned - that was until she met Charles. The alluring, mysterious Charles. The lying, reticent Charles. She still didn't quite know what to think of the man yet, but one thing she knew for sure was that he had caught her attention in a seemingly unusual way. A part of her was actually looking forward to her next meeting with him.

***

Her knees gave way as she looked up at the man; his face a blur. Her gun sat in the holster against her waist, but she couldn't reach for it, she couldn't even move a finger. Her head slammed face-first on the table as she flopped down on the carpet. A blood-curling shriek rung out in the air and she wanted to reach it. *She had to reach it.* A hand forced her face down hard. The alcohol burnt at the base of her throat when she cried out in vain. The cries from another room continued as the man behind her leaned against her ear, his words barely audible against the screams and the ringing in her own head.

"It's all your fault."

Madison's eyes shot open as she scrambled down the chair she was settled in, her hands desperately fumbling for her gun. Her fingers hit the lamp that was perched on the table facing the sofa and it dropped to the floor, shattering to pieces. The sound was enough to bring her to her senses, and she slumped down defeatedly on the floor, wedged uncomfortably between the sofa and the table. Rubbing her tired eyes, she let the reality of her surroundings sink in and felt the loud thrumming of her heart against her chest ease.

Over the past few months her new prescription pills had made her dreams vivid; her terrors often leaving her scrabbling for her gun. It was a good thing that she had taken to keeping it in her duffel underneath her bed. She was certain one day she would find her way there in a languid stupor and shoot something, or someone, down.

The phone vibrated against her thigh but she decided against taking the call. She stiffly wondered if it was from the Peterson kid - calling off the promise he had made to her earlier that afternoon about not involving law enforcement. She didn't have the emotional capacity to deal with a lawsuit, or a sullen kid for that matter.

Whoever it was, she would deal with it the next morning. Now, however, all she wanted was to crawl into her bed, toss back another sleeping pill and pass out until her body's internal clock shook her awake at sunrise.

But the phone rang again. This time she pulled at it, shooting a weary glance at the mess she had just made.

She picked up the call, placed the phone between her ear and her shoulder, pushing herself up.

"Yes," she mumbled, nimbly pulling the carpet away from under the shards of glass glistening in the nightlight.

"Madison?"

It took her a moment to recognize the voice. "Phil?"

"Hey...I know it's late, but can you come up here?"

"Right now?" She glanced up at the wall clock. It was past two in the morning.

"Yeah. Th-they, uh, they found a body!" Madison stopped dead in her tracks.

"What?"

"Yeah. There's so much happening, Madison I…"

"Wait, where? Where'd they find the body?"

"Close to the property, by the sinkhole."

She rubbed her face with her free hand. Phil sounded like he was barely holding it together. This was not how she had planned to spend the night.

"They think it's a woman but it doesn't even look human anymore. Just please - get here as soon as you can. Please."

"Of course. I'll be there in an hour."

***

It took longer than an hour because of the horrendous rain. The sound of it beating down against the roof of her car was deafening, but she paid little heed to it as she drove up the empty highway.

Karl had called her a few minutes after Phil, sounding frantic as ever.

"I swear it's one of those loons from the hunting clubs."

"I doubt that's the case, Karl," Madison had offered firmly when, in reality, she was still in a daze. She wasn't aware of Lyndhurst's crime rates, which she hoped was a good thing, but she couldn't completely count out the possibility of it being a murder either.

"We don't even know how she died yet," Madison had told him.

"Probably a bullet to her head," Karl had helpfully suggested.

He should hope so. If it turned out to be an accident his business was going to take the fall for it.

"You know what, I'll call you when I reach Elwyn."

"Hold on, hold on! Please find out what's happening there. I know it's a lot to ask, but can you please do this for me? I cannot have the commission upbraid me again for this."

"Fine! I'll try."

6

The first thing she noticed as she drove in through the main gates of Braytons' Riding School was the plethora of police cars parked in the driveway. Lights loomed through the tree lines in the distance as uniformed police officers hurried about and around a very distraught and pale-looking Phil. His tall form stood by an empty parking spot. Clad merely in a pair of crumpled sweatpants and a buttoned-down cardigan, he was drenched to the bone but made no attempts to seek shelter from the rain.

Relief flashed across his exhausted face when he saw Madison pull over in a spot close to him.

"You okay?" she asked as he stalked over and planted himself next to her car.

He nodded frantically. "Just never been… this shaken up before."

As Phil led her to the tree line, crowded by policemen and equipment, he filled her in on what had happened. Six Legs League, a local hunting club, were out on their nightly pursuit of game - hoping to take advantage of the freshly stabilized barometric pressure after the continuous rain. Instead, they stumbled upon a grotesque-smelling corpse at the bottom of a four-year-old filled-in sink hole.

"The pit must have opened up again because of the rain this week. There's no other reason we could've missed it," Phil muttered to her as they made their way through the forest towards the fence-line.

When they finally reached the site, Madison realised a part of St. Elwyn's ancient fence-line was swallowed up by the freshly eroded extension of the pit. Blue tapes sealed the place off, but anyone could've made out the giant hole on the ground from afar. The sickening smell of rot hung heavy over the dewy petrichor.

It was then that she caught sight of the zipped-up body bag; its lumpy contents joggled as a pair of officers carried it away. A sight she had once grown used to as an ex-homicide detective and one she had desperately wanted to distance herself from the last few years.

"DCI Sharpe?" a familiar voice called to her. She turned to catch DI Rashid Tudor making his way towards her.

"Detective Tudor," she said with a smile.

"It's been so long – how have you been?" he asked incredulously.

"You two know each other?" Phil queried.

"Of course, we do! DCI- oh, pardon me! Miss Sharpe had been our overseer for a whole year. She was a legend in the Organized Crimes Department. We learned quite a bit working under her supervision."

Phil wordlessly nodded to that, the displeasure blatantly evident on his face. She felt somewhat defensive at his reaction, but she was sure that Karl had spared him a few details about the time she had hit rock bottom a few years ago. But given Phil's current circumstances, he was entitled to his aggravation, just this once.

"I've been well. I'm guessing you're doing pretty well too."

"Funny you say that, ma'am. I'm just weeks away from getting ahold of that promotion, finally."

"Should be the case. It's about time you did," she said with an acknowledging nod to the guy who blushed in response.

She remembered Tudor quite well. Mostly because he had quite the tendency to differentiate himself from others; most of the time unintentionally so. In the beginning she had misjudged him to be the quiet and naïve kind who would shy away from law enforcement after a couple years, but it turned out that his quietness was purely calculative, for he only ever offered his opinions when he was dead sure about something. In which case he was probably right. His most discernable trait was his insane imagination, thanks to years of being exposed to crime television.

He grinned. Embarrassed and at the same time visibly pleased by her words.

"So, what do you think?" she asked.

"We…" he glanced uneasily at Phil and then back at her. "We suspect it was a suicide."

"Oh God." Phil momentarily recoiled at his words but then spat back instantly, "You people told me it was an accident!"

"I clearly remember adding a 'probably' before that, Mr Graham. And we had initially thought that. The body is terribly mangled from the fall, but there are distinct marks on the wrists that should not result from a fall of this kind."

"What kind of marks?" Madison asked.

"Seems like the volar parts of her wrists were torn off, flesh and all, by what we suspect…" Tudor gave Phil another uneasy glance, "human teeth."

Phil turned around, having had enough of the conversation, and walked back towards the clearing.

"Just give him a little time."

"Of course," Tudor said with a firm nod.

"So, she bit herself off and then jumped down the pit?" she challenged.

"Hard to tell. But from the looks of it, that's what we suspect happened. I'm sure the post-mortem will confirm it." He glanced out at the route back to the clearing. "What a way to go," he added thoughtfully.

Madison hummed in agreement.

"How long do you think she's been down there?" she asked as Tudor led her to the sinkhole.

"Around a week. The smell certainly gives that away."

The sight of a man in dark robes enshrouded by the thick fog lingered at the back of Madison's mind.

"Any chances of it being foul play?" she asked.

"Hm?" he stole a worried glance at her, taken aback by the question. "We don't have reason to suspect that... *for now*."

"But?" she pushed.

"I just - I think it's a very, *very* elaborate way to end yourself. If I'm lucky we'll identify her, find a suicide note somewhere and that'll be that. And if I'm even luckier," he passed Madison a guilty smile, "I get to make a case out of this; one that would get my investigative juices flowing."

"Cold bastard." Madison scoffed.

"I'm just saying, a murder case would look great in my file," he reasoned. "This is it," he gestured towards the inside of the pit.

They stood unnervingly close to the opening. The muddy soil still shifted inches away from their feet and Madison found herself backing away on impulse. A careful peek inside the dark crevice informed her that the bottom was filled with murky water, sloshing wildly against the sides of the pit, freeing more of the soil and debris into it. She could barely make out the bottom of the pit, even with the dominant police spotlights planted around. Rocks and debris jutted out dangerously along the eroded sides, slowly sliding down towards the sinkhole's churning center.

"How did you get her out?" Madison muttered.

"We almost didn't! Thankfully, her leg was stuck in the mud when we found her. It almost slipped out by the time one of our officers got to her."

Madison grimaced and turned away. "How long will this take?"

"We're almost done. Not that we can find much in this weather anyway. In another ten minutes we'll be out of Mr Graham's hair."

"Good. I'll go see how he's doing."

"How do you know Phil Graham then?" Tudor asked abruptly, falling into step with her as she wove her way back to the clearing.

She glanced at him and considered the obtrusive question for a moment. That's right, Tudor had always been the heedlessly invasive kind, somewhat like herself, which made her wonder if he was on to something.

"Is this an interrogation?"

"No. Just curious." He pursed his lips for a moment before saying, "You must be quite close considering you're the only person Mr Graham called in."

She shrugged. "He lives alone by the heath. His family are overseas and so are the Braytons. He probably doesn't have many people to call during emergencies."

Tudor merely nodded. As they reached the clearing, the Braytons' residence stood proud and alight in the midst of the surrounding darkness, seemingly warding off the foreboding vehemence of the rapidly worsening weather. The wind howled and rain lashed down heavily on them as they made it to the house.

They found Phil in Karl's office, speaking to someone on the phone. Standing across from him was a female officer, equally drenched as the rest of them, waiting for Phil to hang up.

Tudor nodded to her and she nodded back.

"Karl will be flying in tomorrow. He told me to hold fort until he arrives," Phil informed the officer sliding his phone in to his cardigan pocket. "That'll be all then," the officer told Phil. "Thank you for your time, Mr Graham." And with that she took her leave.

"That's Officer Agatha Palmer. She's heading the CSI unit. Don't mind her, she's not one for introductions," Tudor informed Madison. "As for you, Mr Graham, I suggest you do not leave the city for a while. We'll have someone contact you as soon as we confirm the victim's cause of death."

Phil's eyes widened in disbelief. "Does that mean I'm a suspect?" he snapped at the other man.

"It's just standard procedure, Mr Graham. Nothing to worry about. Unless you have something to worry about," Tudor replied soothingly. "You don't look too well. Do you have someone you could stay with tonight?"

Phil looked to Madison for help. His tired eyes pleading to her earnestly. She nodded. "I'll be here."

"Well, since that's settled I should be on my way as well," Tudor concluded with a professional smile, and stepped out.

"Tudor," Madison called after him, following him out to the

foyer. He stopped in his tracks and turned around. His eyebrows raised curiously at her approach.

"Can I ask a favour?"

He looked genuinely taken aback by the request. "Of course."

"You might not be authorised to do so, but-"

"Let me guess, you want me to keep you informed about this investigation," he smirked.

"Will you?"

"As you said, I'm not authorised to divulge case-related information to non-personnel, but... I will be more than pleased to bend the rules for you," he added with a grin. "I've never spoken to you up-front like this before today," a trace of nervousness crept into his voice, "and I *have* to say, it's been rather nerve-wracking. You are a legend in our department."

"I'm flattered, DI Tudor."

"We were devasted when we heard of your resignation, ma'am. But I would be lying if I said I didn't see it coming, right after you lost your-"

"I understand," she said interrupting him. "Thank you for that. But I think I'll be needing your number."

Tudor looked disoriented for a moment at the interjection, but he was quick to recover. "Of course!"

They exchanged contacts and Madison sent him on his way before she was pitied any further. Conflict avoidance, she thought back to Charles Fincher's words about his uncle; she could use a bit of that in her own life.

She found Phil gazing out of Karl's office window. Having sensed her arrival, he snapped out of his daze.

"I'll take the guest room. You get some rest while the sun's still down," she told him.

"Thank you for staying tonight."

"Of course."

He looked sickly pale and panicky. A state Madison would never have expected to see him in. A part of her almost missed his usual cool demeanor. "Her face. I… I can't get it out of my head," he stared at Madison. "When they called me out there, I thought to myself how bad could it be? But then *I saw her*," his head rocked from side to side.

That amount of time in the water is not good for a human corpse. Madison could only imagine how horrible it had looked and felt genuinely sorry for the man in front of her.

All Madison could do in that moment was quietly hold his gaze. She had no words to offer him, no way to comfort him. Because nothing she did would make him unsee what he had already seen, nothing could soothe over the effects it had on him.

"I don't think I can sleep tonight," he mumbled and turned back to the window.

She left Phil at Karl's office and retired to the guest room. But she didn't expect to get much sleep that night either.

***

She woke up at dawn. No dreams had haunted her that night and, to her surprise, she'd slept quite peacefully. Glancing out the window next to the bed she saw that the fog had returned over the fields and the surrounding forest. She wondered if the sun had yet to come up fully or was it to be another dull day.

Her feet carried her downstairs and out the front door of the Braytons' house. She tried to be as quiet as she could, wary of the fact that Phil might still be awake in the office room.

Unlike the previous night, there was no wind to dissipate the thickening fog and she felt claustrophobic, even though she was outdoors.

She strode towards the tree line eyeing the dense murk that still covered the tops of the towering oak trees.

Nothing moved. Nothing made a sound.

She trudged along until she could make out the gray pavement of the parking space. Her weather-beaten Bronco was the only car in sight.

She was stood on the exact spot she had seen the figure about a week ago, hiding right beyond the final line of oak trees opening into the clear field.

He'd have had a clear view of her, seeing that she could even make out her car number plate from that distance.

She walked deeper into the forest, picking a path through the trees at random. The mud padded the sound of her boots and even the soggy grass refused to scrunch under her feet. The only definitive giveaway of her ever being there would be her footprints, but they would be of no match against the autumnal showers.

She stopped at the blue and white police tape surrounding the sinkhole.

Tudor mentioned the woman had died around a week ago. Possibly around the time of Madison's last visit to the ranch.

She had been told it was a suicide, but she doubted it. Although, her seeing a figure doesn't amount to anything. Especially as she had good reason to doubt herself.

She figured time would tell, at least that's what she hoped as she wove her way back to the house; this time at a much quicker pace.

She found Phil in the office asleep on Karl's swivel chair. Bags lined his eyes and his lips were chafed and bloody, even so, he looked peaceful in his sleep.

She placed a blanket over him and wrote a note before leaving. Police would be swarming Karl's house and Karl himself would be arriving later that day. She had no reason to stick around longer than necessary.

***

Madison's phone vibrated just as she entered her apartment. Letting the door fall shut behind her, she accepted the call from Allison.

"What?" Madison uttered, dropping her jacket on an empty hook of the coat rack by her front door.

"Good morning to you too," Allison chirped on the other end of the line. "I have some intel on your man."

"Go on," Madison urged as she strode over to her kitchen to pull out a sweeper and dustpan.

"As I guessed, he is fifty-two and currently settled in New York. There isn't much on his family, which I found odd, and obviously points to the fact that he has taken measures to dispel any such attempts at profiling him. As for his business, he works as a property developer. And, apparently, has just recovered from bankruptcy. He owns a house in Georgetown and lives alone - according to an Ad for a lawnmower that he posted on craigslist three months ago. Fortunately for you, your man has a LinkedIn profile, and I suggest you contact him through that to appear less dubious. He seems like a twitchy guy."

"And how do you know that?"

"He adds about sixteen ellipses at the end of every sentence on his posts. He is either eighty or has a lot of repressed emotions. And I know that he isn't eighty."

Madison scoffed. "Fine. Mail everything to me."

"Already did," Allison chirped before cutting the line.

Madison checked the time. It was only seven in the morning, which meant she would have about an hour to spare before she left for Esher.

She clomped back to the living room, sweeper and dustpan in hand, only to find that there was no mess for her to clean. Her umber carpet was neatly laid out on the floor, in its place next to the center table; as if it had never been moved. No broken lamps or shards of glass lay in sight and even the cushions atop the couch she had fallen asleep on just hours before were neatly arranged.

She stood riveted to her spot by the kitchen door, staring at the tidy living room, wracking her brains for a probable explanation.

She didn't recall cleaning up before she left for Lyndhurst the previous night…

She shot back inside the kitchen and found the broken remains of the lamp dumped inside the bin by the counter.

"This doesn't make sense," she muttered to herself.

Her phone buzzed. Tearing her gaze away from the bin she saw Elizabeth Fincher's name flashing on the screen.

We're leaving in an hour. Wait for Henry by the gate when you arrive, the text read. She distractedly eyed the message as a sense of unease came over her.

"Stop doing this to yourself," she told herself, aloud this time.

She had a busy day ahead of her and Madison decided there was no time to waste on her pointless paranoia.

After a quick shower, she forced herself to eat a slice of toast as she locked up and jogged towards her failing, dull blue Bronco. However, she showed it no mercy as she slammed the door shut, buckled up and screeched off.

She reached Esher at a quarter to nine. Having to stop twice to dry heave by the roads - the toast hadn't budged from her stomach, and she felt somewhat triumphant about that. Leaving the Bronco in a discreet spot of a supermarket carpark, Madison jogged to the Fincher Mansion.

Henry waited for her by the giant metal gates that led into the property. His characteristic, emotionless expression offered her a simple nod on her approach.

He led her to Charles' office with an unfazed indifference that almost bordered on boredom. She could hear the clinking of dishes coming from the kitchen and guessed that the rest of the house staff were still on duty.

Henry tried the door with his gloved hand, but the handle wouldn't budge. At a moment's notice, he produced a small blue screwdriver from his trouser pocket. He jammed it into the keyhole and turned it around, making the lock click open.

Pushing the door open, he gestured for her to enter.

"I'm not allowed in," he declared, taking his place next to the door as Madison entered the dark room. A rather respectable gesture from a man who just broke into his employer's office.

The black curtains drawn over the tall bay windows barely let in any daylight. She felt around for a switch in the darkness and found one right next to the door. As she flipped it on a huge structure at the center of the room lit up. With a start, she realised it was an oversized glass display, the kind you see in museums, holding archeological discoveries and taxidermic animals. Golden lights glimmered from all its edges, bright enough to illuminate the entire room. On closer inspection she realised the base of the display case was covered by, what appeared to be, a patch of dense green grass. Paintings stood atop, some fixed onto easels and some left leaning against the glass. Also in the cabinet was a white chair holding yet another set of paintings. A rather peculiar decoration to have in your work room when you're a multimillionaire on the verge of bankruptcy, she thought.

As her eyes adjusted to her surroundings, she noticed there was not much to the room aside from the luminous glass case. A four-poster bed stood in one corner - in front of the covered windows and wedged between a pair of short wooden nightstands. There was a desk stood in the corner opposite to them but she wondered if Charles had a tendency of standing around because there wasn't a single chair in sight, not even a desk chair; none but the one locked inside the glass chamber.

That wasn't enough to faze Madison, what did unsettle her, however, was the number of sticky notes covering the walls. From phone numbers to addresses and names circled in red, as well as writings in different languages scribbled onto the notes and even on the bare plaster of the wall. Parts of the dull grey wallpaper had been ripped off to make room for more angry scribbles, and it was clear that it was no sane man's doing.

She stepped away from the walls, taking in their deplorable sight with a sense of rising alarm. She wasn't supposed to see this. No one was.

Rummaging around the desk, there wasn't much to see except for a laptop and an untidy stack of newspapers. The unlocked drawers were empty except for a few yellowing bills from a furniture company named 'Glasgow Furnishings.' She tried the laptop next. Placing her thumb against the camera, wary of any security system Charles might have setup on it. The screen came to life as she pressed the power button and was greeted with a lockscreen. She'd expected as much. She couldn't guess the password and doubted Henry, or even Elizabeth, would be of much help.

A glint of light caught her eye and she turned to peer at the far, darker end of the room on the other side of the massive glass case. She discovered that what she had initially thought to be a wall was actually a pair of doors painted the same gray as the rest of the room, the golden light from the case seemingly reflecting off the surface of a pair of steel handles.

She reluctantly walked across the room, her eyes still surveying the mess on the walls in the scanty light. Her hands found the steel handles and she slid the doors apart. Bright lights escaped the room. With shelves and shelves of garments and accessories lining the walls, she had discovered a walk-in closet. Madison undid the laces of her boots, tossed them aside and took a step inside the closet. Her bare feet landed on the soft fur carpet that instantly impressed under her feet. She wondered if Charles would notice the extra impressions of feet the next time he was in there. And with that thought, she took to the sides, walking only on parts of the floor that weren't carpeted.

A strong musky aroma of lavender hung heavy inside the room, one that masked almost every other scent in it. She noticed incense stick holders on the island of drawers along with a powdery residue lying around them and guessed they were to blame for the strong miasma. The deeper she tiptoed down the great passage of Charles' closet, the stronger the scent grew. The incense stick holders now atop every shelf and island with some even stood on the floor between the clothing racks.

Searching through every drawer and cabinet, Madison came across more irrelevant papers and documents that she tucked back into place after going through them.

After a strenuous hour of searching through papers, receipts, and organizers stuffed underneath clothing or inside cabinets, she stumbled upon a framed picture of a child. The little girl was draped in a big dusty coat. Her face smeared with soot, she jauntily beamed up at the camera with a toothy grin. Madison noticed the girl looked very malnourished – her boney cheeks were sunken and bags lined her eyes, although she seemed oblivious to her condition and looked rather happy as she posed for the picture.

Madison noted the time stamp marking a corner: '07:11:96'. She idly wondered if she should try that as the password on Charles' computer.

Putting the picture back in its exact place, she glanced around the closet. An ivory curtain covered the far end of the wall, where she stood. She pulled the curtains away in the hope of seeing daylight, but all she was met with was a pair of tinted glass doors. The handles to which were fastened in place by a chain lock.

Squinting through the glass she discovered it was in fact another room; a very dark one at that. She could barely make out the walls inside it, much less its contents. But she could just make out an odd square on the floor right in the middle of the unusual room. It looked an awful lot like trapdoor, she thought.

A knock resounded. "Miss Sharpe, I suggest you speed things up! It's already noon, and Mr and Mrs Fincher are on their way back!"

"Uh… I'll be done in a minute!" she yelled, pulling the curtains back in place over the glass doors and rapidly making her way out.

"Zero-seven, eleven, nine, six," Madison muttered, typing the numbers into the password box on the lockscreen of Charles' laptop. It unlocked instantly. She was taken aback for a moment, blinking at Charles' beaming face on the wallpaper. He didn't look much younger in the picture, but much happier than how he had seemed in person the other day. His hand was possessively draped around a surprised Elizabeth who appeared to be shying away from a shallow wave of water, but she seemed happy as well. Less polished, but definitely happier.

A sense of sympathy arose in her for the couple, but she shrugged it off.

A clump of minimized tabs sat on the taskbar. She started clicking them open one by one, only stopping when she spotted something even minutely relevant to her case.

One of the many tabs was a spreadsheet of some sort. Which, on closer inspection, she realised cited transactions from various bank accounts made within the month. She changed the starting date to 1st January 2019 and set the end date as 30th November and pressed enter. The page refreshed and a new list loaded onto the screen. She scrolled down and hit the 'save' button. As a copy of the spreadsheet saved itself onto the computer, she opened Charles' email and let out a gleeful laugh seeing that he was still logged in.

Her eyes widened as she scanned the lines of emails from a certain 'S.K.'

Simon Kane, no doubt.

And by the looks of it he wasn't deterred easily. Seemingly, he took the time to send Charles an absurd number of emails every day, some written professionally while some blatantly threatened him with the worst consequences.

Time was precious, which made it impossible to go over all the emails individually. But as far she could tell most of them were from Kane. One of the few not from him, was from a 'Matthew Harper, MD', confirming an appointment that coming weekend.

She composed a new email from his account, dropped the copy of the spreadsheet onto it and typed in the address of one of her many anonymous accounts. Just as she was about to hit 'send', her eyes landed on a peculiar email in Charles' inbox. It was not from Kane and it didn't have a subject-line, but it had been opened before. The sender's address was a collection of random numbers and letters. Biting down on her lip, she clicked on it.

The door to the office creaked. "I really suggest you speed things up in there, Miss Sharpe," Henry's voice echoed through the room. She didn't fail to notice that he had used her real name instead of the one she had offered to Charles. Maybe Elizabeth had already informed him of her true occupation and identity. If Elizabeth trusted the man, she could too.

The body of the mail was empty as well, except for a time, a date and possible coordinates of a place. Clicking on the numbers, a map of an area in Shoreditch popped open. Most places in the area were unmarked and consequently finding a recognisable landmark nearby was out of the question. Instead, she took a picture of the email with her phone.

She eyed the date: '08-22-19'

Late August. About a month before the supposed disappearance of Fincher's money from the account.

She closed the email and gave the newly composed mail a final once-over before clicking send. She cleared all traces of her using the laptop and wove her way back to the door.

As she reached for the switch to turn the lights off on her way out, she gave the unusual display case a final glance. Her eyes widened at what she saw.

Faint smudges marked the glass, that she distractedly thought looked very much like scratch marks.

7

Back at her house, after gazing blankly at an old telecast of a beauty pageant on her muted TV, Madison finally willed herself to open the copy of the spreadsheet she'd managed to purloin from Charles' laptop that morning.

She had doubts about the legality of fishing through someone's computer without their consent, but since Elizabeth - Charles' state-appointed guardian *and* wife - had allowed access to it she guessed it would be fine.

Her eyes were bone dry by the time she had gone through every individual transaction listed up to November that year. She flopped backwards onto the mattress of her bed.

Pulling the pillow from her lap, she slipped it under her head and closed her eyes.

It's no use, she thought.

She'd managed to trace some of the accounts back to luxury clothing stores and fancy restaurants, most others, however, she'd failed to find.

As a yawn tore through her open mouth she wondered if she could get in touch with Elizabeth's consultant.

Before she knew it, she had drifted off. Until she opened her eyes to the sunlight seeping through the blinds of her window.

She didn't get up though.

Instead, she stared wide-eyed at the ceiling. Silently recalling the sight of deep green pupils, and the long lashes lining almond eyes, as their gaze had burnt through her only moments ago. She recalled familiar broad lips gently moving to form words that were silent to her ears. But somehow, she knew what was spoken. Her own name. Over and over again, with deep fondness.

It felt real. Yet it was nothing more than a dream.

The dread bubbling within her was almost crippling. She felt still and empty but at the same time panicky and impatient.

Her phone buzzed against the dresser, breaking her daze. She hauled herself up and grimaced at Elizabeth Fincher's name on the bright phone screen.

"I was expecting a call from you at the very least," Elizabeth's cheery voice filled the other line.

Oh, I was busy dreaming about your husband actually, an impish part of her brain tittered in her head.

Instead, she hit back, "I was getting to it." She glanced at the clock by her dresser. It read 7:03.

"Well, actually I'm glad you didn't. Charles seemed rather… *healthy* last night and this morning come to think of it. I didn't want him worrying for no reason," she panted into the phone. "Pardon me, I'm out for a jog. It's a lovely day and an excuse to get away from the house this early without looking suspicious. I've been dying to hear from you since last night."

Madison rubbed her eyes. "The only thing noteworthy I found is a spreadsheet on his computer, listing all of his transactions from various accounts."

"A spreadsheet?" Elizabeth asked. "A bit… straightforward of him, no?"

"My thoughts exactly. Which makes me think that Charles has nothing to hide after all."

"I really hope that's the case," Elizabeth sighed.

"Do you think you could send me the statements?"

"I've been meaning to ask. Have you tried tracking the transactions on his accounts?"

"Why would I do that? The money went missing from a savings account we only use to pay our staff at our Boston house. The only money we use from it is the chunk Charles transfers into it every other month. *And* I'm familiar with most of the accounts charging it."

"You didn't see anything out of the usual?"

"Nothing noteworthy, no. I can send you the list of names if you want."

"I think that might be helpful. Also, do you think you could have the bank track other transactions too, from his other accounts?"

"Yes. I think I can manage that. Although I reckon it'll be a waste of time."

Madison paused briefly. "I think it's worth a try. I'll let you know if I find anything else."

"Looking forward to it."

She wondered if she should ask Elizabeth about the large glass chamber, but thought better of it. The smudges could well be from a house staff or Charles himself. Someone had to get in there to clean up and perhaps the scratches were made accidentally.

When Madison was in the shower she missed a call from Rashid Tudor and a text from Phil that read, *Still mad about you leaving without a word.*

She hadn't heard from either of the men since the night the

body was found at St. Elwyn. Which was about three nights ago. She had however received a call from Karl who was very distressed about the size of the sinkhole. Luckily it had stopped growing, and after an inspection from a foundation specialist it was ready to be filled-in again.

She would have to visit him soon. Give him updates about the police investigation that she herself had yet to receive.

She returned Tudor's call, who picked up after a single ring.

"I didn't want to bother you until I had something solid," Tudor informed her sheepishly.

"That's fine."

"I think I'd prefer doing this face-to-face. Do you know somewhere we can meet?"

She considered the question for a moment.

"How does The National Gallery sound?"

***

"We'll be moving onto another incredible piece by one of the founders of the French impressionist movement, and the father of impressionism himself - Oscar-Claude Monet. This," the guide told a group of school students, gesturing to a painting of two women at a beach: one looking out into the distance, the other busy with a book, "is The Beach at Trouville."

"The lady in white is Camille Doncieux, first wife of Monet and the one in black is Madam Boudin, wife of Eugene Boudin, who was also one of the very first French landscape painters and a lifelong friend to Monet."

"I don't get paintings," Tudor muttered, eyeing the framed paintings littering the wall. "I respect that they were very innovative in their own timelines, but I'm simply not fascinated by them."

"I saw you leering at the Caravaggio painting a few minutes ago," Madison informed him.

"That's because mutilated heads fascinate me," Tudor replied candidly. "Criminals too."

A few of the students from the group stole perturbed glances at them, while the guide shot them one of pure displeasure.

Madison scoffed and decided they should move on to the next room.

"You see that?" she said pointing to a larger painting, depicting a blindfolded woman in a white silk dress. One man guided her gently to an execution block, while another held an axe. The other two women seemed mournful, one even facing the other way, as if appalled by what was about to take place.

"There's nothing inherently wrong with the painting. No apparent bloodshed or gore. But you know it feels grim. You know something bad is about to happen. The implication itself is sometimes much more horrifying than the actual act," she analysed, turning to him.

"Poor Lady Jane Grey," he lamented, frowning at the index plate next to the painting. "She died for deeds of her father. Most don't even know who she is. Were you always interested in European art?"

"Not really. I'm researching for a case," she informed, eyeing the rows of meticulously detailed oil paintings.

"I thought so." At first she thought it was just him being smug, but by the approving smile on his face, Madison realised how impressed he was by her answer, almost as though she had proven her worth to him again.

"Why don't you bring me up to date now, Tudor," she plopped down on a nearby empty bench. He took a seat next to hers, without losing his frown.

"Well... we looked into the missing person's database and obtained several visual matches on the body: dark hair, south Asian, five-feet tall, fairly common features. Her body was a bit bloated, but still recognisable – not too bad considering she was down there for a while."

"Were they able to ID her?"

"No," he shook his head, "the FLO brought in about twenty people and no one could recognize her."

Madison frowned. "You got any pictures of her?"

"Yes," he said, pulling out his phone.

She looked as good as a week-old corpse would, but her facial features were fairly discernable as compared to her body from her time in the water. Madison could see why Phil had been so shaken up that night.

"The teeth marks on her wrists match her own and were made prior to her death, but she didn't die from pulmonary oedema, like in most drowning victims. She died from internal bleeding."

Madison's eyes widened at his words.

"There were signs of blunt force trauma to the back of her head, her chest, her stomach and she had a broken nose. She was severely malnourished, and we also found traces of ecstasy in her system. We don't have a proper timeline, but my guess is that she had been abducted and then... murdered."

"She was buried, but the sinkhole set her loose?" Madison offered sceptically.

"Yes. Probably," he said with a nod. "Karl Brayton and Mr Graham might be called in for questioning tomorrow. We already have search warrants issued for the hunting clubs surrounding the site of discovery, since they frequent the area more than anyone else."

"Will this affect Karl's ownership of St. Elwyn?"

"As long as it wasn't an accident, which I don't think it is, he'll be fine," he assured grimly.

Madison nodded. "Well," she said after a while, "at least you got yourself a nice murder case to add to your file."

Tudor chuckled at her tone. "Yeah, I suppose I do."

She turned back to the painting, wondering if Tudor would let her know of his proceedings with the case any more than he has to, since he wasn't obligated to do so in the first place. But she could really use the distraction once in a while.

The whole Fincher case seemed bland and drawn out in comparison, and a part of her longed for the zeal she felt during homicide investigations.

When she resigned, she never thought she would miss her job, especially after what it had cost her. But her mind had been moulded to take pleasure in her work. It was either that or the complete collapse of her sanity altogether. And once upon a time she had willfully chosen the former of the two.

She didn't leave the museum immediately after Tudor did. She walked back in and paid the admission fees again. "I'd like to take a guided tour this time," she told the man behind the counter.

Her guide was a man who seemed to be about her age. When she told him to lead her to the 18th to 20th century works first, he readily agreed. He delved deep into what was deemed prominent in the time period and offered valuable insights to their worth in the later years.

"I see the Monet piece interests you," the guide, Lukas, commented. Madison tore her gaze away from the painting to look at him. "It does. Although I don't really know much about art, I quite like the way he portrayed sceneries. It lacks details but at the same time it seems so awfully… detailed."

"And you've just defined impressionism. Detail without details. Creating complex scenes through minimal detailing. Subdued, yet very precise. His work doesn't always suit people's tastes though."

"I can't imagine anyone disliking them."

"It's less about disliking - more about the general misinterpretation of his skills. He was heavily criticized during his time as an artist. He had cataracts and critics used his failing eyesight to demean the value of his works.

"That caused him to destroy a lot of his paintings in frustration. He once said that his life was nothing but a failure. That he planned on destroying his paintings before he disappeared. Today he is considered to be one of the greatest painters in the history of the world; his paintings deemed as priceless evidence of humanity's success."

"He'd have been happy to be alive today," Madison lamented.

"Not if he found out what a good lot of his paintings had to go through during the second world war."

Madison looked up questioningly at the man.

"Thousands of artworks were looted or confiscated from Jewish art collectors in France alone by the Nazis. Monet's paintings hadn't been immune to the rampant theft. Some of them were destroyed, some were lost - never to be seen again, and others that survived the whole ordeal were luckily recovered."

"How many of his works are accounted for as of today?"

"Let's see… around two-thousand five hundred of them have been found. There are plenty that have been reported missing during the war, as well as in recent years. We keep them in an archive, and hope that one day they'll turn up!"

"How many of those are privately owned?"

"Plenty of course. Are you looking for anything in particular?"

"I recently came across a family that owns one of his paintings from the eighteenth century. An unnamed item and I suppose that piqued my interest in his works. The family claim that no one has seen the piece before. I'd like to find out more about it, but they want to keep its existence a secret."

Lukas considered that for a minute. "Maybe you'll discover more about it in the archive," he suggested. "Monet didn't name all of his works, but if you could give me a date, I could narrow the list down for you."

"That would be wonderful! Would you mind if I contact you at a later date?"

"Of course not!" he said, pulling out his phone from his pocket. "I'm not really supposed to give my information out during work, but just this once should be fine," he offered with a wink. "For the sake of art."

8

"I'm telling you; Powell is a prat who wants to get rid of me," Karl spat bitterly on the other line. "I bet he prays for it every Sunday Mass. Gets off on my misfortune every night."

"Oh, shut up!" May yelled, from somewhere in the distance, causing Madison to break into a fit of laughter.

Karl grumbled at the interruption.

"C'mon, you're buddies with Powell. He even got you that little bow-set on your birthday," Madison reasoned.

"That's one of his old ones. It got rusty so he gave it away to me, trying to win my favour. It broke a month later, after the riser rot off."

"It broke because you couldn't use it and still tried to shoot a buzzer with it," Madison argued. "Don't go hating on him just because he gave you an odd look."

"Oh, but it wasn't just him! Alfred, Bones, Earl and even Peggy! And I know what they were talking about when I stepped into that darned bar this evening. That Powell is spreading lies and turning everyone against me, and I'll have the skin of his back for it! I've got enough on my plate as it is between that corpse and the bloody hole, last thing I need is him riding my back."

"What kind of lies did Powell spread?" Madison asked, sensing the shift in the man's tone.

Karl often lashed out violently at unpleasant situations in an attempt to hide the grief he felt. Despite his hard appearance, he was soft at heart. He still felt like an outsider in Lyndhurst, regardless of the time he had spent there. This often caused him to be unusually sensitive during even the most minute social altercations.

"Those buggers think I let some blonde prat stay at my place. The bloke apparently stole from their club and ran away. But I think it's nothing but a clever ploy to drive me out of this darned forest."

"Did you let someone stay over that week?" Madison asked.

"No! Only Phil. Apparently, the blonde bloke told them that he was staying at my house that week and wanted to hunt with the club that weekend. But he vanished a few days before the hunt."

"Did they tell the police about him?"

"They did apparently. The police don't think he's related to the case. Although they probably think he's made-up too."

"What did the man steal?"

"An air rifle I think, and I heard something about a machete, or maybe a crossbow. I haven't had the chance to ask the club, you see," he added sarcastically.

"I don't think you should worry too much about this, Karl. Get some rest. You'll have to go down to the station tomorrow, and that'll be quite taxing."

Karl grumbled.

Madison felt sorry for him. The recent events had been hard on him, but she was glad that at least he wasn't alone, and had May and Phil to rely on at a time like this. She wondered if she could make a quick trip to Elwyn later that week, but a familiar sense of uneasiness filled her, and she thought better of it.

Later that afternoon Madison scanned through the lists of transactions Elizabeth's consultant had mailed her. The sources were tracked and listed in alphabetical order. After hours of scrolling through the names, and looking them up online, she found nothing suspicious. But she still had a long way to go.

When she finally decided to take a break the sun had already set.

A cold breeze drifted in through the open windows in the living room, it carried with it the scent of wet soil which made her wonder if it had drizzled again. The cold sent a chill down her spine, but the scent felt pleasant.

She fixed herself a quick snack and settled back down on the warm couch. The TV was silently playing a noir movie she wasn't paying any attention to. She never paid much attention to things playing on it, but kept it turned on for the sake of a distant sense of normalcy.

Even as she stared at the screen her mind was elsewhere. She was thinking about her planned visit to Elizabeth's place again the next day.

She wondered if she would get more out of Charles about his uncle this time, or about the painting. But for that to happen she would have to appear trustworthy to him. This could be tricky since Charles Fincher was virtually unreadable. Even if he was somehow convinced that her red-headed humanities student persona was somewhat reliable, he wouldn't give any of it away on his face.

She was yet to have another dream about him since that first time, but she still felt uneasy about facing him again.

She grabbed her phone and found the picture that she had

taken of the subject-less email on Charles' computer. She typed in the coordinates on her own computer and the familiar map of Shoreditch popped open on the screen. There were no markers in sight, other than the untagged one the coordinates pointed to. If she were to move along Boundary Street up to a place called Cavalier Avenue on the map, she could find the exact point denoted by the coordinates.

It was definitely worth looking into. She could even make the trip that evening, since it was only a thirty-minute drive from Soho.

***

She made the foolish mistake of underestimating the traffic in Chinatown – again.

What should've been a thirty-minute drive ended up being a sixty-minute one.

But the farther she drove, the more sceptical she became. Following unsubstantiated leads was not something she was fond of, but this and Elizabeth's transactors' list was all she had at the moment. However, she was aware that the chance of her finding anything worthwhile that night was small.

When she finally reached Shoreditch she left the car at the end of an empty footway. The streets were quieter than she had expected, but as she followed the route to the single marker on her map, the area grew increasingly emptier still, until there was no one else around.

She pulled up her hoodie and kept her head low as she marched. Shoreditch wasn't a great place to be alone at night and her five-feet-five form couldn't exactly fend off someone with a weapon, especially if they were to take her on by surprise.

The route led to a long graffiti-covered alleyway, wedged

between two unmarked warehouses; none of which seemed like they had been opened in a while. Packing boxes and old plastic bottles littered the area.

Only a dimly lit streetlight stood at the far end of the intersection which did little to dissipate the darkness in the alley. She couldn't make out what was on the other end of it.

Switching her flashlight on she took a cautious step. The water leaks and the sultry weather made the alley damp and suffocating; the pavement grimy and sleek. The stench of urine and vomit only added further to her misery.

As she reached the end, all that welcomed her was the sight of a bare brick wall and a couple of reeking dustbins. Rats skittered away upon her approach as she eyed the map on her phone informing her that she had arrived at her destination.

She scoffed at herself but froze when she heard footsteps against the wet pavement behind her.

"Can I help you?" a feminine voice asked her.

Madison spun around to see a woman of average height in a puffer jacket, staring at her questioningly. It took Madison a moment to realise that she was looking at a very familiar face.

"I was told to come to this marker," Madison said, showing the woman the map on her phone.

The woman, however, didn't seem interested in it. "Are you here to buy a painting?"

A painting?

Before she could say no, Madison stopped herself. "Yes…" she stammered instead.

The woman raised her brows meaningfully. "Come."

Madison did not doubt that the woman in front of her held an uncanny resemblance to the unidentified body found in St. Elwyn.

The woman in front of her was, however, much taller than five feet. Her hair was up in a messy bun, tied in place with a yellow bandana, which made her look even taller.

Madison followed her down the street and around the line of partially constructed buildings. They arrived at a busy street lined with pubs and other old-fashioned dives. Queues of people stood outside the clubs, waiting to get in. Some of them curiously eyed the woman in front of her as she passed them, one even making an obscene remark at her, to which she casually flipped them off.

The woman came to a halt in front of a small antique shop further down the street. It had tinted glass windows and bare-bricked walls. The woman held the door open for Madison to enter, and as soon as Madison did, her nostrils were assaulted with the strong scent of lavender. The same kind she had inhaled in Charles' closet.

A South Asian boy, who looked to be in his early teens, stood at the front counter. He regarded them with disinterest for a moment and then returned his attention to the magazine in front of him.

"She wants to buy a painting," the woman said as she closed the door behind them.

"Yeah? What kind?" he asked without looking up.

They both spoke with a thick accent and bore similar facial features, making Madison wonder if they were related.

"What do you recommend?" Madison asked, taking in her unusual surroundings. The only source of light inside the shop were the uncountable string lights hanging from the ceiling.

Items of all sizes adorned the shelves of the shop. Some looked old, some relatively new. White mannequins dressed in oriental clothing were scattered around the small store, alongside massive intricately decorated trunks and boxes. A giant grandfather clock, occupying one of the walls, ticked loudly over the pop music playing on a portable radio sat on the counter, next to which a half-burnt stick standing on a thin copper stand emanated fragrant smoke. A narrow staircase ran to an upper floor, on which she spotted a stack of white canvases.

"Can I see your ID?" the woman asked.

"We sell legal drugs too, you know?" the boy said with a hint of annoyance to his voice.

And at that moment, Madison realised what 'a painting' actually meant.

What kind of illicit drug dealer demanded identification? she thought to herself.

The woman told him to shut up in English, followed by words in a language that Madison failed to catch.

The woman held out a hand to Madison. "ID," she demanded again.

Madison handed it to her. The woman gave it a thorough examination before returning it to her. She locked eyes with Madison for a moment as if trying to read her. "We have some Molly, or do you want some of the stronger stuff?" Her casual tone reminded her of her ex-husband, Paul, when he used to ask her if she wanted Pizza or Pad Thai for the weekend treat.

"She's obviously here for the stronger stuff," the boy spat, flipping through the magazine.

"Yeah… no, I think I'll back out. Can I get something legal instead?"

The boy scoffed.

"I stood in the cold for *three hours*. Are you serious?" the woman demanded, her already thick accent growing even thicker as she spoke. "The Datura stuff is so good too. It's such a waste," she added, turning to the boy who paid her no heed.

"Sorry," Madison said. "I came down here in a moment of weakness, this was a bad decision," she tried to sound as convincingly miserable as possible.

The woman narrowed her eyes at her. "What do you want then?"

"I'd like some speed if you have any," Madison said, looking away from her and at the curved metal staircase leading upstairs instead.

The woman rolled her eyes and stomped over to the back of the store, disappearing behind a curtained doorway.

"Are those paintings?" Madison asked.

"Yes. We sell actual paintings too," the boy said, flipping over a page.

A convenient cover, Madison thought.

"You interested?" he asked.

"Yeah. Can I take a look?"

"Sure," he answered distractedly.

It seemed that the entirety of the top floor was dedicated to an overwhelming array of paintings – some piled up, some fixed onto walls, some eased onto stands. She didn't have to be an expert to tell how beautiful and detailed some of them were.

But one painting in particular caught her eye. It depicted two women, one in white and the other in black.

She knew the painting well. It was Claude Monet's 'Beach at Trouville.' The same rough brushwork, the similar monotone colours, his familiar art style from the eighteenth century – except this wasn't hung up in a museum, but in the attic of a quirky antique shop.

The uneven patches of dried paint on the painting informed her that it wasn't just an original print. "It's a fake." Madison turned to see the woman standing at the stairway. "Done perfectly."

"You sell forged paintings?"

"Oh, no. That isn't for sale. We do rent it from time to time. There are a couple of others too."

"You painted this?"

"My sister did."

"Is she around?"

"No. Here's your speed," she held out a small packet of white powder.

Madison hesitantly received the packet from her. Madison had so many questions, and yet she couldn't bring herself to ask any. It wasn't the right time.

"There's two grams in there. That'll be fifty," the woman informed her.

Fifty pounds for two grams of amphetamine was grossly overpriced, but Madison had no choice but to comply. She felt for the wad of bills in her pocket and pulled out a fifty and another twenty by mistake. But before she could put the extra bill back, the woman wrenched her hand back up and powerfully pulled both notes out of Madison's grip.

"The twenty's for backing out," the woman glared at her with a toothy grin.

Her eyes were big and pea-shaped, lined by long thick lashes. Her broad, convex nose suited her face well, as did her long black hair, that she had rearranged, now out from the bandana and to her shoulders in thick wavy locks. It tremendously complimented her brownish complexion and her roundish features. And for a quick moment, Madison was transported back to the dense forests of St. Elwyn. The woman seemed bigger now, her once beautiful face bloated and broken. The deep brown of her pupils had been replaced by a sickly bluish-white, and her hair clung to her sickly skin in a ropy tangled mass. Her skin no longer retained its beautiful bronze sheen and instead appeared pallid and rotten.

The corpse would give a rookie pathologist nightmares for at least a week, and yet Madison knew that it had once resembled the vivacious and youthful woman standing in front of her.

Madison opened her mouth, and yet all that came out of her was a passive, "Thanks."

She didn't face the woman again and calmly walked downstairs and out the shop door.

9

"Ooh, vanilla," Allison sang as Madison placed a pot of ice cream on top of her desk.

"For your good work," Madison praised as she flopped down on one of the chairs. She almost guffawed at the look Allison gave her at the rare clement gesture.

"Do you have a fever?" Allison asked, genuinely concerned.

"Don't get too used to it," Madison said with a grin.

"I'll try not to," Allison replied, mirroring Madison's grin. "So, what can I do for you today?" she said, reaching for the ice cream.

"I need you to look up the owners of an antique shop down in East Shoreditch. It's called 'Days of 49'."

"Catchy name," Allison remarked offhandedly as she typed the name into her computer. "Found it," she declared after a minute. "It has a three-star rating. Oh, this one's funny. 'Don't go unless you want to get mugged,' Moira Cara from Birmingham writes. I'll see what I can find."

"Thanks, and uh… hey…"

Allison looked up from the screen. "Anything else I can help you with."

"Do I- do I look… sick to you?"

"Uh... not sick per se. But," Allison looked confused. "You kind of do, I guess," she added with a frown. "But I thought that's what you go for. You know, the lethargic, irritable detective who also happens to be very sickly. Why?"

Blunt, audacious candour. Madison expected nothing less from her brusque assistant. But Madison couldn't bring herself to face her. Instead, she found a small crevice on the wooden desk and started scraping it with her nail.

"I was mistaken for an addict last night."

"You what?" Allison's voice inquired in outrage.

"It all happened very... spontaneously. I had little time to react and had to play the part to avoid discovery," she poured out, her face warming with each word.

Her eyes found Allison with a hand pressed against her mouth. "It must have been an honest mistake." Her words came out shaky and muffled under her hand.

Madison almost smiled at Allison's attempt to keep herself from bursting out in laughter. But she had only confirmed what Madison had been told many a times before, and what she already knew herself.

"Did that... *offend* you?" Allison asked after sucking in a sharp breath and removing her hand.

"It did catch me off-guard," she confessed. "I mean, I'm aware I haven't been taking care of myself as well as I used to."

"I don't think it's too bad. I mean, you could try doing something different with your hair. Or maybe try wearing some lipstick."

Madison glowered at the woman. "Get to work, Miss Day."

"Yes, Ma'am," Allison complied with a grin.

***

Madison had never let her appearance bother her, and she had no intention of letting it bother her now. Yet she couldn't take her eyes off her own reflection in the mirror. It was like looking at a train wreck – an awfully repulsive sight, yet she couldn't look away.

She had never been thin. In fact, she was quite chubby in her late teens. But now, as her bony fingers traced the skin of her chest, grazing against the protruding bones of her rib cage, she felt a sense of alarm tingle through her mind.

How could she have lost that much weight without noticing?

In her defence, she never spent much time in front of the mirror since she resigned. She didn't have reason to. And Harry didn't care much for appearances either, so she'd never had to put much effort into the way she looked. Quite frankly, she didn't have the extra energy to spare.

Madison's own mother had hated her freckles. They covered almost every square inch of her skin, and she had been raised to hate them too. She had always thought that they stood out rather viciously against her pale skin and now they seemed even darker than she remembered them to be.

The smell of coffee filled her nostrils as she smeared the concealer on her skin – carefully covering the brown and orange spots tainting it, dabbing in just enough product to divert attention from her spots.

She put on a brown knit sweater and a pair of black jeans. She towel-dried her just-washed hair and forced her stubborn curls up in a bun.

Returning to the mirror, she gave herself a final once-over and admitted to herself that she looked better. Happy even. The concealer did a great job at hiding the shadows underneath her eyes, and in making her cheeks appear fuller than they actually were.

Surprisingly, the lipstick hid her chapped lips under a layer of deep red, and her normally wild hair seemed settled in place for a change.

She didn't feel any different, though. But she was hopeful that she would later in the day.

On her arrival at the Finchers' house she wasn't escorted in as usual. Instead, they let her car in through the gates, and she found her way up to the house.

She heard muffled voices as she stepped into the hallway, where no one stood to receive her. She let herself in and followed the voices down a corridor, through the living room, which, in turn, led to a dining area separated by a perforated wall partition.

The couple hadn't noticed Madison's arrival and did not make any attempt to curb the tone of their conversation.

"Why?" Elizabeth spat.

"Cause I'm not sick," Charles offered calmly. He was seated at the table, and his focus was on the newspaper he held. It was evident that he had little interest in what Elizabeth had to say.

"But you are Charlie!" Elizabeth countered, her voice rising a full octave. "You left me to handle everything by myself. The least you can do is admit that you are sick. That you need help!" She appeared close to tears.

"I've said this before. I'll say it again. You don't have to handle it if you don't want to," he defended nonchalantly.

"Take your medicine, Charles, while I'm still being nice," Elizabeth warned.

She didn't wait for a reply. She closed the distance between them, wrenched the newspaper out of his grip, and hurled it to the floor.

"What was his name, again? Stephen? One of your pals from

that conceited little boys club of yours. Yeah, I know about your little conversations about me," she spat. "He thinks I'm unfaithful, and," she let out a scoff, "and so do you."

"After everything I've done for you," she let out almost in a whisper, as she shook her head in disbelief. "After everything we've been through together, you have the audacity to doubt me."

"I really do not appreciate you eavesdropping on my conversations," Charles muttered as the fingers of his right hand tugged at the unbuttoned sleeve of his left.

"HOW DO YOU EXPECT ME NOT TO HEAR THEM?!" she shrieked. "I have to tag along everywhere you go like your bloody governess, terrified of you ending up doing something stupid - something irreversible - something your friends will have my head for."

Charles shook his head in anger, but was confused by Elizabeth's claims. "That is not true," he muttered. He appeared to be at a loss of words, "I… whatever Stephen and I talk about does not concern you. I suggest you go back to bed and stay there until you're summoned."

"Who- WHAT?" Elizabeth gaped at the man in disbelief. "Who are *you* to dismiss me?" she spat. "I am no longer your ward, Charles. I am your wife," she reminded him through gritted teeth, her nose scrunched in defiance and disgust. "How long do you plan on living in denial - acting like you're perfectly fine?"

Charles turned away, feigning disinterest as he leaned down to retrieve the scattered newspaper sheets from the floor.

"You," she slammed a small plastic cup on the table in front of Charles, stopping his movement, "don't get to ignore me." Her voice was impressively steady for someone with tears of rage streaming down her face. She grabbed hold of his hand and forcibly moved it to the cup.

Charles appeared to freeze at the contact. In moments, the air around him changed.

He eyed the disposable medicine cup for a moment. "Take your hands off me," he said in a chilling voice.

"No, Charles, I won't."

He regarded the hand gripping at his wrist with an unreadable expression before leaping to his feet, knocking his chair down. And before Madison had the chance to react, Charles' fist slammed into Elizabeth's face, instantly knocking her backwards. Her back hit against the marble counter behind her with a loud thump.

An agonized cry left the woman as she grappled for her bleeding nose.

Footsteps and screams of alarm rolled through the house as the staff rushed to their aid, but Madison's feet were already carrying her to the couple before anyone else.

Madison threw herself between the two before another strike landed.

Which… it never did.

When Madison looked up at Charles, barely registering Elizabeth's cowering form, her own hand raised to ward off the man.

Charles seemed as surprised at Madison's reaction as she was herself, his eyes widening with horror and confusion at his actions.

He pushed his hands to his chest as if to bring back control over himself.

"You're not even half the man you used to be, Charles," Elizabeth hissed miserably, her voice broken and muffled under her palm. "You're only a pathetic shell!"

He stumbled backwards and fell to his knees. Shock and disbelief flashed across his face. "I didn't… I didn't mean to," he sputtered, attempting to crawl away from them and the violent consequences of his own actions. "I thought you were…"

"Sir," Henry called as he rushed over to his master's side. "I'll get him upstairs," Henry informed as he hauled the shaking man up by his elbow and guided him out of the dining area.

Only when the two men had left the room did Madison register the frenzied shrieks from the woman behind her. Her fingers were clawing at Madison's sweater as she screamed obscenities at her husband.

10

The sun was dwindling as Henry drove a teary Elizabeth to the local hospital. Her nose – twisted at an odd, painful angle – was undoubtedly broken.

At the Finchers' house the staff had returned to their posts leaving Madison to her own devices. She had planned on leaving after seeing Elizabeth go, but a strange sense of anticipation kept her from doing so right away.

She knew Henry had put Charles to bed before leaving. He certainly wouldn't be able to meet her in the condition he was in, and she wasn't sure if she should face him after his aggressive display. But drawing on her understanding of people living with dementia, it was clear to Madison that Charles' seemingly aggressive behaviour was a direct result of Elizabeth's antagonistic behaviour. He had lashed out at her because she had provoked him.

But a sick part of her still *longed* to meet him again. And she hated herself for it.

The man was losing control over his actions. The confusion and fear in his eyes had made that clear to Madison. He was well beyond his mild cognitive impairment stage, and much graver things awaited him and his wife.

Madison felt that Elizabeth's limited understanding of the

symptoms of dementia were to blame for the unfortunate events that had occurred that afternoon. Charles' condition may be deteriorating, and Elizabeth is failing to manage his needs sensitively. Both had fallen victim to a situation that Madison wouldn't wish upon even her worst enemies, and both needed time to heal from their altercation. Madison was witnessing a family on the verge of breaking apart.

She distantly recalled the picture that was still set as the wallpaper on Charles' laptop and hoped there was still a chance for them.

She thought back to the separation from her own husband. There wasn't any illness or missing money involved, but they had still broken away from one another; despite their love for each other. And with time that love had also dissipated.

Madison was alone in the living room again, staring blankly at the tapestries on the wall opposite her.

"What am I still doing here? I should leave," she said to herself in a whisper. She had outstayed her welcome after all.

An older woman in a black uniform entered the room. With wrinkles lining her face and neck she looked to be in her late sixties. Madison remembered Elizabeth referring to the woman as Carla, earlier that afternoon.

"Miss Murphy?" she asked.

"Yes." Madison replied slightly startled.

"Mr Fincher would like to see you."

"Me?" Madison asked, feeling a sudden tightness in her chest.

"Yes. But if you don't feel like it…"

"Uh-no. It's okay. I'll see him."

"Well then, please follow me."

Madison thought she was being led to the office room, but instead, she was ushered into a separate bedroom right across from it. She kept herself from stealing a glance at the locked door to the office room, where she had been just days before.

The bedroom was spacious but smaller in comparison to the office and presented a rustic décor; complete with bare brick walls and straw furniture.

Charles was settled on a wooden stool next to the bed, his feet propped up on the mattress. His white renaissance shirt was wrinkled, and a stain of blood marked his collar.

"You're late," he informed her pleasantly.

His welcoming smile bore no traces of the distress that had sullied his handsome face only hours ago.

She looked to the maid, who simply smiled at her confusion. "Would you like me to bring up some of our fresh brew for you and the madam, Sir?"

"Yes, Carla. That'd be splendid," he said.

"I don't drink coffee," Madison supplied hastily.

"Oh. I didn't know that. Tea then?" Charles asked.

That confirmed her suspicions.

"No. I'm fine," she replied.

"Then I'll just prepare a cup for you, Sir," Carla offered and took her leave.

"How are you, Miss," he hesitated for a moment, as if trying to recall her name, "Murphy?" Charles inquired as he idly played with the strings hanging from the neckline of his loose shirt. "You seem a bit tired. Did you have a tough time at your previous engagement?"

Despite the pleasantries that he sent her way, Madison couldn't help but notice that Charles appeared jumpy.

"Yes," she replied. "You could say that."

"Explains why you were so late," he said, getting to his feet.

He moved around the room and drew open the curtains to

reveal a small balcony. Two chairs and an easel stood on it, and the canvas fixed onto the latter was turned away from the room, hiding it from her view.

"But it's alright now," he concluded strolling towards her. The same green eyes that she had dreamt of only a night ago now locked onto hers. And she couldn't look away.

He positioned himself in front her, and she unconsciously parted her lips in anticipation.

His hand reached up to tuck away a stray curl from her temple behind her ear. "I take good care of my guests," he admitted, almost in a whisper.

He smelled nice, she thought. A heady mixture of aftershave, sweat and…

Lavender.

Suddenly, very aware of their close proximity, she took a step back.

She read the same awareness in Charles' eyes, and he retreated his hand as well.

"I have something to show you." An uncharacteristic shyness seeped through his features that surprised Madison.

She sensed hesitance and tension in him - the kind that contradicted his usual confident demeanour.

Just hours ago, this very man had hit his own wife, yet now he stood flushing in front of a stranger, stripped clean of all his defences and aggravation. He didn't attempt to close the distance between them again. Instead, he reached for her hand and gently led her to the balcony. "I've been looking forward to our next meeting," he stated with a smile.

He picked the canvas up and turned to her. He held her gaze before slowly turning the canvas around to reveal the completed works.

It took her a moment to realise what she was looking at. Bold dark strokes of different colours merged in a peculiar yet gorgeous depiction of a face. A series of odd flamboyant spots littered the canvas in place of freckles on the face which she knew very well was her own.

"I don't know why, but I couldn't get you off my mind after our first meeting," he confessed. "Sometimes I recall your name, and then there are times I don't. But you… your face wouldn't leave my mind alone until I brought you out on a canvas. I didn't know if you'd like it, though. I'm aware that it's unusual to have a stranger paint you without your permission, but it was the only way I could put my mind to ease," he rattled off. Madison couldn't help but wonder if this excitable version of Charles was how he used to be in his younger years. She almost smiled at the thought.

She didn't know what to say or how to react. All words failed her as she gazed at the beautiful painting of herself.

"I'd like you to have it. Or it's yours to give away in case you don't like it," he said.

"No. No, it's… beautiful," she eventually spoke. "I can't stress enough how beautiful this is," she added, looking at the fretful man with the blood stain on his shirt.

"Well, that is a relief," he said, the smile returning to his face.

"I just - I didn't expect this," she said. "We've only met the once. And to be able to create something this incredible after a single short meeting is," she shook her, "disturbingly brilliant." She let out a laugh.

Charles beamed. "Oh! I have no doubts about that. I am indeed very disturbed," he said, tapping a finger against his temple, "up here."

Madison smiled, her eyes trailing across the browning stain yet again, and the smile slipped away from her face. "Mr Fincher, why don't we talk for a while?"

"I would like nothing more. Have a seat," he gestured towards the straw chairs.

By the time Carla had brought in the coffee, Madison and Charles had already progressed from their initial niceties to more trying topics like Madison's childhood.

"I think you owe me a few more meetings before we get to that," Madison said. There was no point in telling him something that he wouldn't remember the next time they met. But she didn't know if there would be a next time.

"I don't owe you anything," Charles pointed out, taking a sip of his coffee. "However, I won't press you to tell me anything that makes you feel uncomfortable. But you did promise me that we'll talk more about you this time."

Madison sighed in defeat. She needed to earn the man's trust, and to do that, she needed to be as honest as possible with him.

"I lost someone close to me… a while ago," she said hesitantly.

Charles' gaze tore away from the view that the small balcony beheld and settled onto her.

"I don't think I've been the same since. Even if I wanted to go back to being the person I used to be… I don't think it would be fair to them."

"Do you blame yourself for what happened to them?" Charles asked.

"I do," she said, feeling the back of her throat burn at the admission. She knew she would choke if she let out another syllable.

Madison found him staring back out at the view, deep in thought. She didn't think he would respond anytime soon and felt flustered at the fact that she had overshared and had made the man uncomfortable - like she had most people in her life.

"Don't," he said, turning back to her. "I don't think the person you lost would want that for you."

Madison gazed down at her palms, glowering at the gentle tremors running down them.

"I mean, haven't you suffered enough?" he said with a humorous smile. "And I doubt that your loved one would want to carry the burden of your trauma with them up there either. Once you let go and stop living in the shadow of your past, you'll learn to forgive yourself."

Madison shook her palms off. "Are you speaking from experience?" she asked.

Charles smiled at the question and gave her a nod. "I felt the same way for a while. But I think I'm okay now."

"Was it because of your uncle?" she asked before she could stop herself.

"Very perceptive, aren't you, Anne?" he said. "Yes. I did feel a certain way about his death. We were very close."

"Was he from your mother's or father's side?" She decided she'd push until he shut her out for good. If that was the last time she was allowed inside the Finchers' house, she was determined to make the most out of it.

But Charles appeared to be oblivious to her determination, and instead smiled cheek to cheek at the question. "My mum's side," he replied, brightly. "My very first memories of him were in my mum's hill house in Cheshire. He was her primary caretaker when she became pregnant with me, since my own father couldn't care less."

"I suppose he was like a father to you," Madison offered.

"No. He wasn't. My father was... well my father. I wouldn't want to compare him with my uncle – or any agreeable man for that matter.

"Uncle Michael was always around. He was there with my mother when she had me, and also at my father's estate working as a part time gardener. For a man as free spirited as him, he had quite the artillery of skills. No job was too big or too small for him. He could do just about everything."

"He was bright and funny and… colourful even," he added fondly. "Can I tell you something unbelievable? You might think that me and my family are complete nut-cases after you hear this – but I think most people already think that anyway."

"Lucky for you, I'm not that quick to judge," Madison encouraged.

Charles let out a laugh at that. "My uncle, he could perceive emotions in colours. And he could recreate those emotions through paintings - to evoke the same in others. Memories, thoughts, sentiments; he could identify all from a mere glance at a painted piece. That way he could point out a lot about a painter's personality and even as far as what the painter was feeling while he created his piece."

"He told me that he inherited this ability from his grandfather, but it usually skips a generation. I presumed it skipped mine and I remember being so agonized by that as a kid. I was so jealous of him that I refused to speak to him for a whole week."

"I'm guessing you got over it," Madison asked, hugging herself against a particularly cold breeze.

"No… I don't think I'll never *not* be jealous of that man. But he told me that there's a good chance my kids will inherit it. That put me at ease for a while. As I grew older I convinced myself that maybe his queer little talent wasn't as wonderful as he made it out to be. I mean, why was it only limited to painting and not digital art? Those are pretty popular too, right?"

"His ability only contributed to his crazed infatuation with paintings. That man, he foamed at the mouth every time he spotted a beautiful piece on church windows."

"He wanted to nurture that same infatuation in me, and he took me to just about every art museum and gallery the country had to offer. Made me learn techniques and art styles and to differentiate works based solely on said art styles."

"Was he successful?"

"Oh yes. By the time I was in my early teens I had some pretty nice brush techniques of my own."

"But Uncle was never the same after my mother's passing. He became colder, distant. My mum's death didn't stop my visits to Cheshire though. If anything, it only increased them. But I often found him brooding in the library and in mum's room, which was unusual considering he was a very sound-minded fellow."

"I stopped visiting the Cheshire house after I turned eighteen. Painting reduced to a mere pass time for me since I was in university. Uncle Michael stopped visiting the estate as well, soon after. I blamed my father for my uncle's estrangement, but it didn't take me long to realise that I was abandoned," he scrunched his brows as if the thought disturbed him.

"I'm sorry," she muttered.

"I'm over it," he insisted, rather strongly, even though his slumped shoulders and the tension in his frame told her otherwise.

He managed a smile. "Well, when he passed away, he donated Mum's place and most of his belongings to charity. He passed down what little fortune he had left to the children of his friends and acquaintances. Only *I* wasn't worthy of receiving anything from him. And I had grown to despise him for it," Charles' voice shook terribly as he bit back a sob. "Until the day of my marriage."

"What happened?"

"He left me a wedding gift. A painting."

Bingo, she thought to herself.

"Isn't that nice?"

"No," he scoffed, staring out at nothing in particular. A crazed look replaced the sorrow in his eyes, "He passed his curse onto me. That's what he did."

"What?"

And just like that, the moment had passed. Charles bolted upright in his chair. His eyes and posture suddenly devoid of all signs of sorrow and warmth that it had displayed just moments previously.

"Carla!" he called out, abruptly standing and clomping back into the room. "Carla! How long has it been since I asked you to bring up the damned coffee!" he demanded at the top of his voice.

As Charles threw open the door and stepped out, unrest from the staff filled the house.

Madison, having been completely forgotten by her host, remained seated in her chair, quietly gazing down at the still steaming cup of coffee resting on the narrow side-shelf of the wooden easel.

11

No matter how morose and emotionally drained she felt, her visit to the Finchers' place wasn't a complete waste of time. In fact, she'd gotten exactly what she had wanted - more information about the uncle and his crazed attachment to paintings. Although, she still didn't know how any of it contributed to Elizabeth's case, yet.

She flopped down on her couch and turned on the TV. The strange goings-on over the last few days raced through her mind. Visiting a place where Charles had supposedly met with someone, days before a huge sum of money disappeared from his account, and encountering a woman who bore an uncanny resemblance to the unidentified body found in Elwyn. If the alleyway was used as a common discreet meet up spot for buyers and vendors, it would make her encounter with the woman nothing but a mere coincidence. In any other case, however, there was a possibility that Madison's case was somewhat linked to Tudors. Maybe Charles had met up with this exact same woman. But Madison couldn't move forward with her theory unless the woman's relation to the unidentified body was confirmed. All she could do, for now, was wait for Allison's call and go through the remainder of the list that Elizabeth's consultant had forwarded her until she reached a dead end, that is.

She rubbed her eyes as she focused on the muted TV, willing herself to get up and get to work, but a sense of indolence kept her from moving. She idly gazed at the newspaper-wrapped canvas sitting on the center table across from her.

"Maybe I should give you away," she muttered to the painting.

She was still stumped by the abrupt change in Charles' behaviour, and wondered if that was the reason behind her sudden state of inertia. Perhaps seeing his symptoms firsthand had made her realise that pursuing the undeniable attraction she felt for the man was futile and pitiful. She had even gone ahead and shared an intimate moment with him only hours after she had watched him hurt his own wife.

If she informed Harry, the boss of the Detective Agency, of her personal attachments with her client's husband and that it was affecting her case, maybe he would allow her to pass the case onto someone else.

"What are you even doing?" she asked herself, throwing her head back against the backrest of her couch and shutting her eyes.

An hour later, she was on her laptop looking through the Finchers' family tree. She had memorised the names of almost every person on the tree by that point, but she kept looking in hope of finding something new.

Charles was born in 1964. According to a few sources, his mother was barely an adult when she gave birth to him. Other sources cited that she was in her late twenties, either way, she was born sometime between 1936 and 1946. Which meant Michael was born sometime between that too. During the war he would have been less than nine years of age. If he had inherited the painting he would've done so from his father. But Amos was a nobody, no one knew who he was or what he did other than the fact that he was a doctor. And perhaps, that was what she needed to find out.

"Elizabeth? Can I ask you something?"

"It's a bit late, no?"

"It'll only take a moment. What do you know about Charles' maternal grandparents?"

"Uh - okay. Hmm let me think... nothing about his grandmother. No one even knows her name. But I think she died during the war. His grandfather, though, I've seen pictures of. I think he came to London right after the war ended. Misha and Sir Rawlins were toddlers when he took custody of them."

"Where was he before that?"

"I don't know. He probably enlisted. No one really knows."

"How old was he when he returned?"

"He looked to be in his forties in the pictures. Why are you asking me this?" quizzed Elizabeth.

"I'm considering all possible connections with Charles at this point," Madison lied. "I'll call you later."

"Uh- okay?"

Madison's research into the missing Monet paintings led her to read all about the ERR, and specifically it's branch: *Dienststelle Westen.* A Nazi operated agency, whose main purpose was plunder, under nicer terms. They mostly targeted Jewish museums and art collections. She came across an article about two individuals named: Josef Lienbelfels and Guntur Einherker. As reported by the Monument's Men, these two raided several museums that were known to keep a wide collection of paintings from Monet and Matisse. A lot of what they stole had remained lost until a groundbreaking discovery on the eve of March 1st, 2013. Hidden away in the basement of a church in Warsaw was a large set of stolen paintings inside an air-tight box.

Madison discovered a link to a press conference under the article. The presentation rolled through several clips of the paintings one by one, as they were revealed to the public. Art that no one knew even existed.

The internet had a lot to offer about the two Nazi officers though. One of the pages had names of all the supposed members of their respective teams that were dispatched to safely transport the looted art. It was there that she came across the name: Amos von Rawlins.

***

"He's got the 'von', which means he was a noble, no?" Allison quizzed.

"Exactly. I think he escaped to here after the war ended."

"And hunkered down with a random lady?"

"He's been here before; he had his children *during* the war. They were around ten when he returned and he probably used them to claim his place here. Maybe he was here during the occupation. I've yet to hear anything about the mother though."

"You think he killed her?"

"I don't know."

"That's really depressing, but I've also got the intel you asked me for."

"That was quick! Go on."

"The current owner is Sabeer Abbas," Allison informed. "A Bangladeshi immigrant whose whereabouts are currently unknown, according to a local, Nancy Polaris' account on a local online complaint board. The woman owns an apartment building near 'Days of 49,' and according to her, the people of the area find the supposed drug trade going on in the shop very disruptive. She writes: '*the little Bangladeshi bugger sold weed to one of my tenants who later, under influence, burned down a whole tree in my garden. When I demanded compensation from them they threatened my safety in the area.*' This woman, she alone wrote around fifty complaints regarding the shop. There are few others about the shop charging high rates for their goods and misdemeanor but nothing noteworthy."

"Looks like Nancy really wants them out of the area – from my time at the place last night, the whole street looks like a typical burnout spot. I'm guessing she has her *own* candy business set up in the area, and there's a good chance that the Abbas' trade was threatening that."

"Candy? Oh, that's code for drugs! Wow. Okay. That never crossed my mind. Anyways, I got in touch with her earlier this evening, posing as a social worker."

"Clever."

"I know! I mean the second she heard that I'm carrying out a welfare inspection in the area next week, she spilled everything – from a broken drain to a group of school students drawing graffiti on her fences. And, yes, she told me a great deal about the Abbas family. According to the word on the street, the father, Sabeer, as I said, disappeared on his family. There are the two sisters: Sara and Afia, who are twins, and Sara's fifteen-year-old son who runs the store. But Nancy hasn't seen Sara around for a while."

"Did she say how long Sara hasn't been around?"

"No… I didn't think to ask. I can always call her up again if you want me to."

"No, you've done enough. And I mean that in a good way for a change. Thanks Ally."

"Oh! Is that a hike I foresee in my salary?" she exclaimed.

"No. I'm afraid your foresight's a bit faulty," Madison replied impassively.

"Aw. Well, good night Boss. Don't stay up too late."

"You too."

She checked the time again. It was 2:27 a.m. She wondered if Tudor would be awake that late in the night, but the answer was obvious. Going to bed early wasn't an option, but a necessity for most field detectives, if they wanted a functioning brain the next day, that is.

All in all, the information she was collecting about the Fincher family was getting a bit out of hand. She had solved the mystery behind the painting, and it's first owner - that turned out to be a Nazi art thief. But she didn't know why her thoughts kept going to Charles' unnamed grandmother.

She bit through to the cuticles of her nails and the sour tang of blood filled her mouth. She grimaced and peered at her severely bitten-down nails. It was either the alcohol or the profuse nail-biting that soothed her anxiety this late in the night, when the noise outside died down and she was left to the mercy of her thoughts. And currently they were speeding through the events of her day and refused to let her concentrate on the names listed on the file sitting open on her laptop screen. When she closed her eyes to let them rest for a moment, she saw the raw alarm and the fear in Charles'. His agonised face slowly merging onto another distant face that rapidly flashed through her mind like blinding strobe lights. She willed herself to open her eyes again but they were sealed shut, or were they? Her eyes were open and she could feel the tears streaming down her face and trailing down her neck to the crook of her ears. And yet all she could see was the horribly pulsating face taking shape in front of her. She opened her mouth but no sound came out. The flashing intensified, burning through her eyes, until she could finally see it: her own face merged and melted into Charles'; colourful goo seeped through the pores of her skin - of their skin, as they both groaned in unison. Their voices miserable and guttural.

When she was finally able to move, she shot out of bed landing on the floor, clawing in desperation for something, anything. When her fingers finally grazed the dusty fabric of the duffel bag stuffed underneath her bed, she grabbed at it and pulled it out. She struggled to get it open so instead, hugged it to her chest until she could feel the outline of a gun pressed against her sternum. Curled up in a ball, she cried until her eyes were red and her throat was sore.

***

"Hey!" Tudor greeted her as he took his seat on the bench next to her. "Did you want some?" he asked, nodding at the latte he held.

"No thanks," she replied, shaking her head.

They were at a community park near Mayfair. It was around eleven in the morning, and the office rush had already died down by the time she hunkered down on an empty bench that faced a tall line of sycamore trees, shedding the last of their leaves.

"You look a bit rough today," Tudor huffed.

"I had a rough night. New medication. Doesn't let me sleep," she offered.

"You should talk to your doctor. Maybe get him to reduce your doses. I was on sleeping pills during high school for a bit. Apparently the dose was too strong for me and I started sleep walking. My dad threw a fit in front of the doctor and had me taken off it," he said, with a humourless chuckle. "The fact that my body could take over control when my brain was out was so fascinating to me. I set up cameras all around the house to see what my body was up to."

"That's definitely very you," Madison smiled. "Thanks for coming down here, by the way, and on such short notice."

"Of course! You told me it was urgent - and that it concerned my case."

"It does. I may have found a lead on the body," she said.

Tudor's brows perked up with interest at her words.

"I had to go down to Shoreditch for a case-related matter and happened to come across someone who bears a very close resemblance to the victim."

"That it?" he asked.

"This woman also has a sister who isn't around anymore. I'm just saying you should look into it."

"Okay…," Tudor swallowed a mouthful of the latte, "that's definitely something. You have a name or a location?"

"I have both," she replied, reaching for the small piece of paper tucked in the pocket of her jacket. "But… I have a condition."

"Go on," he urged.

"If you do find any connection between the woman and the body, there's a good chance that our cases might be linked, to an extent. And I could use your help if that is the case."

"Meaning, the help of my resources?" he said with a smile.

"Yes. That too," she admitted.

"Well, if she does lead us somewhere then you and I, we might have a deal."

"Very well." She handed him the folded piece of paper with the necessary details.

They sat in silence as Tudor went through them.

"Can I… ask you something?" he asked, tucking the note into his pocket.

"Sure."

"Maybe I'm out of line to say this, but why don't you come back? It hasn't been that long since you quit, and I honestly think the PI industry is beneath you."

"I can't. Not because I don't want to go back, but simply because I can't."

She could feel Tudor's stare as he attempted to break her words down.

He finally heaved a sigh and rose to his feet. "Well, I guess I'll see you later then."

12

She eyed the painting sitting on the small sideboard cabinet overlooking her entryway as she locked the door behind her. That morning, before leaving to meet Tudor, she had carefully unwrapped it and placed it next to her faux plants. Its bright colours serve as an unforgiving reminder of her previous night's dream, not that she could ever bring herself to forget it. If the constant comments from her associates wasn't enough indication of her dwindling health, last night's dream paired with the sleep paralysis was indicative enough of that. She had received mandatory professional help during her previous case as a homicide detective. And she had managed to say all the right things to the therapist to get herself deemed as fit to return to the field to work the case. She couldn't afford any interruptions taking up her time back then, and for a good reason.

She made herself a cup of coffee and a quick breakfast and got to work. There were about five hundred pages in the file listing all sources the Finchers' accounts had been in contact with in June and July. Most were irrelevant, others gave Madison an unexpected window into Charles' life.

He was a regular at an inexpensive local cafe. He paid for a particular breakfast order almost every day at about nine in the morning and for a not-so-frequent lunch order from a fine-dining restaurant every other week. He would get a round of coffee from the same café later in the day as well.

Even though his daily regiment was often subjected to change, what remained absolutely firm was his habit of regular payments at the café every morning.

Madison also discovered that he had a love for expensive cufflinks and paint from a shop in Istanbul that manufactured colours from natural pigments. Most other payments were business-related and mostly irrelevant.

After hours of going through the never-ending list, the one name that stuck with her was 'Glasgow Furnishings.' A name recurrent in the vast inventory of the Finchers' expenditures in the year, and one she recalled seeing on one of the very yellowing bills in Charles' cabinet.

Many payments of unsuspicious amounts were made to this establishment, which was obviously a retailer of home accessories from its name. She wondered if this was the source of all the leathery furniture and elegant decor littering the Finchers' mansion.

She thought it would be best to call Elizabeth to ask her about it.

"It's an old furniture store that Charles adores. But I doubt he's ever bought anything from there. I think he usually buys presents from there to send off to his many ex-clients."

And yet, when Madison looked it up online, she found close to nothing about the store.

An address in London did come up and a phone number, but there were no sites dedicated to the store, pictures, or even customer reviews of the place.

She called the number and was directed to a recorded

advertisement of TV packages. She ended the call and eyed the address again.

Maybe it's gone out of business, she thought to herself. There were no other numbers so she looked up the address and discovered that there were no such localities in London as the one mentioned.

All her searches had come up empty. If there were such a store, that had presumably gone out of business earlier that year, she would've found at least a mention of it on the internet.

She looked it up on the publicly available government database of all registered companies in the UK. And, surprisingly, there were seven responses for the name 'Glasgow'. Only one located in south London, named 'Glasgow Furniture and Fixtures,' and it was founded by a Hiram Schmidt. She looked through the very limited details the site offered, and what she saw made her double-take: The store had gone out of business nearly twenty years ago. Another quick search told her the shopping complex in which it had been located had been demolished and renamed a long time ago.

"A paper company," she muttered to herself. She typed in the name 'Hiram Schmidt' and the results were in the thousands. There were too many people named Hiram and Schmidt on the World Wide Web. But one search in particular amused her more than the rest. A link to an article named: 'The Inelegant Downfall of Charles Hiram Fincher.'

***

"What does that mean?" Allison asked Madison, who leaned against the wall next to the only multi-function printer in their building. They were in the waiting area for clients. But since most of their clients usually reached out to them online, the waiting room had become somewhat of a lounge area for the workers. Only Allison, Madison, and the receptionist, Mary, were present in the average-sized room at that time of the day.

Mary had earplugs in and bobbed her head to the music as she worked. Allison, however, lounged on the long worn-out leather couch with her legs propped up, lazily flipping through a magazine she had balanced on her crossed legs.

"It means that this was a straightforward case to crack," Madison said as the printer grinded out a piece of paper next to her.

Allison sat up at the that. "You're done with the case? Already?" she asked, surprised.

"I hope so," Madison offered over the loud constant clicking from the old machine.

"What? Is the serenity of working financial fraud cases boring you already?"

Madison chuckled. "I still need to confirm a few more things."

"Well then, what do you have there?" she asked, gesturing to the set of papers sitting on the output tray.

"Some paperwork." Madison smiled at her.

"You're deliberately being vague, and I hate you for it. By the way, Nancy called me earlier."

"Still waiting for that inspection?" She retrieved the papers and rolled them together.

"No. In fact, she called to thank me. Apparently, the cops came by and arrested Afia Sabeer last night."

Madison turned away from the printer; a look of horror on her face. "And you didn't think to tell me that until now?"

"Well, I'm telling you now! And I honestly thought you had something to do with the arrest," Allison said defensively. "If anything, I thought *you'd* be the one telling me about it."

Madison groaned as she pulled out her phone and pressed

down hard on Tudor's name.

"Hello," he answered.

"You arrested Afia?" she shouted as she darted back into Allison's empty office slamming the door behind her.

Tudor sighed. "She resisted interrogation and tried to flee, which made her appear pretty guilty. Also, her appearance is another thing, the resemblance to the body is simply unavoidable. She's not a suspect yet, but it's not looking good for her unless she talks."

"Did you find out if she's related to the body?"

"We're looking into it. But listen, I can't tell you much, not yet. Officer Palmer's on my back, and if she finds out I'm feeding you information again, I might lose the case."

That wouldn't do. That wouldn't do at all.

"Look, Tudor, I understand. But Afia spoke to me a few nights ago about her missing sister, and I think... I think I can get her to speak. Just let me come by for a bit."

"I don't know."

"Please...Tudor."

Tudor was silent for a moment before a weary sigh left him. "Fine. I'll talk to Palmer. But I can't make any promises."

"Thanks, Tudor."

All Madison could do was wait.

Waiting. That's all she'd been doing all along. She couldn't go out to the field to actively investigate because she would be getting in the way of Tudor's investigation, neither did she have the necessary resources for a case she based around a mere hunch.

Last night, she had stumbled upon an exciting find - an article recounting Charles Fincher's glory days and the unimaginable extent of his success in the short period of two decades. But it also had, rather indelicately, described his steady decline in the latter half of the recent decade, which, according to the author of the article, was brought about by a series of absurd and foolish decisions.

For instance, in March of 2015, Fincher Corporations had decided to invest in a business venture that was 'bound for failure'. The daring feat was extensively publicised, as was the venture's colossal but foreseen failure. It caused the corporation to lose assets worth ten million euros. But a company as resilient and big as FC was sure to get back on its feet, and it did. Only to crumble back down a few years later when Charles approved the manufacture of a new product.

A mere six months before it was set to launch, a popular American company launched a product identical to FC's. FC's product was reduced to a mere fart in the wind by the time it was launched, with its inferior design and complicated features. This rendered irrecoverable damage to the corporation's credibility.

The author had claimed that Charles had gone senile at an early age, and what little of FC remained should be sold off while he could still 'make a buck off it'.

What surprised Madison even further was the latter half of the article. It delved deeper into Charles' background to explain his unusual deficiencies. The author spoke of his father, Hedrick Fincher, in a way one would describe a villain. Born to wealthy parents, Hedrick was spoon-fed the grains of ambition at a very young age. He was the fifth and youngest child in a family that followed a system of primordial primogeniture. He was set to inherit the scraps of his family's lucrative oil business. And so, he had to kill his way to reach the top.

Although, none of it was proven, considering the death of his siblings had all been 'natural' or as a result of being at the wrong place at the wrong time. His eldest brother had died as a result of peritonitis. The second and the third eldest had seemingly died after being caught up in a shoot-out close to their university. And his only surviving brother had spent the remainder of his days in a mental home after suffering from an unknown disorder that would end up taking his life.

As the only surviving heir, he officially inherited the family business at the age of seventeen. He turned it into a far-reaching multimillion corporation in a matter of three decades. Despite being a Fincher, he was more commonly known by his matrilineal surname, Schmidt, or more notoriously Hedrick 'Necrotic' Schmidt, for he brought death to whoever dared to oppose him.

He insisted on being a Schmidt until the rumours about him orchestrating his siblings' death subsided. And it wasn't until his fifties that he switched back to being a Fincher.

It was around then that Hedrick married his fifth and final wife, Misha Rawlins. The young daughter of an unremarkable doctor, Amos Rawlins. But the public already knew Misha as the beauty in Michael Rawlins' paintings. She was her own brother's muse and a sought-after model to several other prominent artists. But her career was cut short after her marriage.

She gave birth to Charles the same year she married Hedrick and disappeared from the public eye. There were rumours that she had developed post-partum psychosis after her last pregnancy and was either sent away or killed off by her husband after she had served her purpose. Both rumours, however, remained unproved, and with time she lost her relevance to the press, and no one really knew what happened to her after that.

Unlike his father, Hedrick had planned on distributing his wealth, and the company, equally among all his sons and daughters, from all his marriage. With the youngest, Charles Fincher, taking on the reigns of the corporation after him, since given his young age he would most likely be the one to outlive the rest of his siblings. And without the need to frequently change heads, the corporation would retain its stability for a long time.

A year after Charles became head, his father was killed in a stabbing at a club he frequented. Gang violence was deemed to be the reason since Hedrick had ties with several prominent gang enforcers. The incident received media attention for a while, but people soon moved on.

And it was then that the gradual elimination of the Fincher progeny began. It started with the youngest Fincher daughter and Charles' elder sister, Rosalie, disappearing during a hiking trip. Her corpse was found at the edge of a steep hill in Australia a week after her disappearance.

The oldest Fincher son, Matias, died from alcohol poisoning less than five years later, followed by the fourth eldest, Klaus, who allegedly took his own life after being unable to cope with the deaths of his siblings.

By this point, it seemed as though the Fincher line was cursed. Out of the three remaining Fincher progeny, two cashed in their halves of the corporation and fled the country in fear of their lives. Charles, who had chosen to stay behind, became the corporation's sole owner.

But when he lived to see fifty, rumours started to circulate that perhaps Charles had been the orchestrator all along. After all, he did have a motive. But the investigations had already ruled out foul play, and there was nothing solid that could get Charles acquitted.

But from Charles' recent failures, the author believes that perhaps Charles was kept alive for a reason and that it wouldn't be very long, 'given his early senility' until he also ends up dead from a 'natural' cause.

Madison had frowned at the bleak conclusion of the article. But was also pleasantly surprised that somebody had managed to keep tabs on the Fincher family even to this day, seeing that the article was published only the previous year.

The rest of the night was spent catching random bouts of sleep in between pondering about the 'Fincher Family Curse'.

She hadn't known about the history of Charles' family before finding the article, and even when she looked it up online she had found close to nothing. They clearly weren't as relevant as they used to be. And all things considered, if the Fincher progeny had indeed been murdered, Charles would be the person to have gained most out of it. A part of Madison didn't want to admit it, but by not leaving as his brothers had, he'd put himself in a rather suspicious position.

She needed to know more before she pointed fingers, of course.

At the office the next morning the door to the office creaked open, and Allison's head peeked in. "You good?" she asked.

"Yeah. You up for some dinner tonight?"

"Depends. Are you paying?" Allison asked, a sly smile creeping onto her face.

"Why not?"

13

The plan was to take Allison to the 'Bibimbap' place behind their office. But what she hadn't expected was the long queue outside it. Somewhere along her day, she had completely forgotten it was a Friday, and most places in the enclave would be ridden with people, more so than usual. Even the cold wind didn't do much to deter the crowd.

"I may or may not have forgotten that today is a Friday," Allison confessed, mirroring Madison's thoughts.

They both stood on the walkway across the street from the restaurant, glumly eyeing the ever-growing queue of people.

"We can always come back tomorrow," Madison offered.

And just when she thought Allison might agree, someone called out to her. "Madison!"

She turned to look at the woman bundled up in a jacket a few sizes too big for her. "Gracie?"

"It *is* you!" Gracie grinned as she pulled Madison into a hug.

A feat that caused Madison to let out a startled "Oh!"

"I thought you were still in Philly?" Madison asked as she pulled away.

"Oh, I'm back for a bit. Landed last night actually."

Gracie Roberts was a former classmate, but they only became

friends in their adult years. She was loud, vivacious and everything that Madison was not. But Madison liked having her around. Gracie, a research scientist posted in Philadelphia for over two years, had lived a somewhat solitary life there. She usually came back once a year to visit her family and would routinely call Madison up for drinks.

"And who might this be?" she asked, peering curiously at Madison's subordinate, who offered an awkward hand to Gracie.

"This is my assistant, Allison."

"Hi," Allison greeted as she shook Gracie's hand.

"Nice to meet you! I'm Madison's old friend," Gracie offered with a smile. "Well, her only *real* friend."

Madison rolled her eyes. "What are you doing out here? And on a Friday night at that. I thought you hated crowds."

"Believe it or not, I had a date. But I got stood up pretty ruthlessly," she revealed with a shrug.

"And since when did you start going on dates?"

"I don't know. I feel like I've been getting lonelier. My mum had arranged this one, though. Booked us a place and everything," she said, blowing into her palms to warm them against the bitter cold.

"What place?" Allison asked with a start.

Gracie raised her brows at the question. "Oh, this tiny Korean restaurant with great ambience near Leicester Square."

"So, did you cancel the reservation then?"

"Oh, no, not yet," Gracie said, shaking her head. "I was thinking…"

"Well, if you don't mind, maybe we can go down there together? You see, Madison promised to take me out to dinner tonight, but I doubt there's any place open that'll accommodate us without a reservation on a Friday night."

Gracie turned to Madison and then back at Allison with a smile. "That's actually a great idea! Let's do it."

Madison grimaced, knowing fully well that she would have to pay for three meals instead of two that evening.

Gracie indeed hadn't lied about the great ambience of the place, though. The restaurant was small and homely. Only a few tables were spread around the bijou area under dim ocher lighting; all of which were occupied.

"So, what case are you working on now?" Gracie asked as soon as the Bulgogi arrived, and she ceremoniously pulled apart her chopsticks.

"You're more interested in my cases than I'll ever be," Madison drawled as she reached for her own set of chopsticks.

"Well, of course! Your line of work is so different from mine, and it feels like a breath of fresh air to me every time I hear you talk about it," she beamed.

"Well, this one's not all that different from my other cases but..."

"But what?" Gracie perked up at her hesitation.

"It's not entirely the same either," Madison replied, shaking her head. "It's really... how should I put it uhh... investing, I suppose."

"It is?" Allison, who was perched on the chair next to her asked. "Why do you come in looking so miserable every day then?"

Madison thought that Allison's inquiry would draw out another backhanded comment from Gracie about her being that way since the day she was born, but instead, the only thing it drew out from her was a fretful frown.

"Okay, well go on," Gracie urged as she idly slurped a noodle through her lips.

"I was hired to look for missing money. Thirty million," Madison exacted in a suppressed tone.

"Thirty million dollars!" Gracie whispered loudly as her mouth fell agape.

Madison simply shrugged at her reaction. "I can't really go into details, but to sum it up, this guy has dementia and has no clue about the money or where it went."

"Oh, that's not good," Gracie said with a frown.

"Well, his wife believes he's lying, but I don't really think he is. Everything about him seems really genuine," Madison pondered.

"So, his wife's pinning the blame on him? You feel bad for the guy, don't you?" Gracie asked fondly. "You have that look in your eyes."

"I don't really know what to think anymore. According to his doctor, he's not getting any better."

"Dementia is an overall nasty syndrome. Though uncommon, I've heard of people faking it when some sort of financial gain is involved or when they want to get out of a bad situation. And commercial drugs aren't all that effective either. It just merely slows down the symptoms. I have a friend from Durham who can help you get more familiar with the effects and the symptoms. Maybe even help you find out if your guy is really lying about his condition or not."

"That will actually help a lot," Madison agreed readily.

Gracie grinned at that. "Wonder where the Soju is?" she breathed out exasperatedly as she sat up straighter. "So, what have *you* been up to?" she asked, pointing her chopsticks at Madison. "You drop all contact with me the second I go back."

"It's never intentional. I can assure you that," Madison

exacted, mirroring Gracie's grin. "I just lose track of things sometimes."

"You just… you've seemed so listless these past few years, it's almost like you're a different person," Gracie approached carefully, with a frown.

"You wouldn't be the first one to tell me that," Madison drawled with a sad smile.

"Does Paul call?"

"Sometimes. To check if I'm alive or not," Madison said with a light chuckle. "Why?"

"I saw him a couple of months ago back, in Philly actually. Did he tell you about that?"

"You did? No, he didn't mention anything. But then again, the last time we talked was a while back," Madison dug into her bowl of Bulgogi. The steam that wafted off the bowl felt pleasant against her skin as she took in the scent of the stir-fried, sauce-covered meat that still sizzled on the porcelain plate.

"We were attending the same seminar, apparently. We talked for a bit but he seemed kind of off, cold even, which came as a shock to me since he was all smiles back when you introduced us," Gracie pondered as she reached for the plate of Kimchi.

"I should give him a call soon. I wonder if he's still in London," Madison mused.

"He's definitely in London. I saw him on the news a couple of days ago."

"Really?"

"Who's Paul?" Allison asked distractedly as she munched on a breadstick whilst staring wide-eyed at the ongoing wrestling match on the giant TV.

"Your boss' ex! Now that I think about it, that seminar was actually conducted by my guy from Durham. Maybe you should ring both of them up."

"What was it about?" Madison asked as she picked a napkin up to rub a stray drop of sauce on her shirt.

"Some Nanotech nonsense. I wasn't really paying attention," Gracie confessed idly.

Madison scoffed at that.

The conversation strayed from there, moving on to the usual reminiscing of their school days and the light-hearted inquiries about their personal lives.

After the three of them parted, Madison hailed a cab back to her apartment. Before long, she was perched comfortably on her couch with a glass of Chardonnay as she checked her voicemail and grunted at the fact that there were still no updates from Tudor or Elizabeth, who had yet to contact her since the day of her visit at the mansion.

She sighed and leaned back on the couch. She wasn't getting anywhere with the case. Gracie was right: an overbearing sense of stillness had taken over her, and it had wholly muddled her ability to think clearly. But she wondered if it was because of the boredom, or the depression. After breaking off things with Paul, she was on antidepressants for a long time. They had been together for seven long years, and a part of her had always thought that he was the one until he wasn't anymore. They had both settled for a break, which in turn strained their already difficult relationship. Although she wouldn't dare admit it to herself, the effects did last.

It was around two in the morning, and she was far from asleep. Her phone lit up and she lazily reached for it. It was an email from Mr Fincher. She frowned at the sender's name and at how her heart raced at its sight. She hesitantly tapped it open.

Dear Miss Murphy,

Today I woke up feeling… good if not great. Although I do believe it has something to do with my wife leaving for Sheffield to meet her parents last night.

Don't get me wrong- I do love her, but with her gone, I do find myself feeling a little less ill and maybe I am a terrible person for feeling that way. She is a kind soul who's doing everything in her power to make me healthy again, and here I am bantering to you about how much I like it when she is away. I'm genuinely pitiful.

But today, I will not do this to myself. I will not drown myself in self-loathing. I'm determined to enjoy this day.

And this determination of mine had me wondering about your book. How is that coming along? I wondered if you would pay me a visit soon and maybe talk more about it. Do let me know.

Charles Fincher

Turning the screen off she dropped the phone aside. She took a big swig from her glass until it was empty. Positioning herself comfortably on the sofa she pulled up a hand to press against her eyes.

It had been a while since she felt this peaceful.

14

Madison awoke to the buzzing noise of her phone vibrating on her nightstand. Still dazed, she'd been surprised to hear the voice of Officer Agatha Palmer upon answering.

"I trust you understand how time-sensitive the matter is, Miss Sharpe," Palmer told Madison the second she'd accepted the call from Tudor's number.

"Yes. I'm completely aware. I'm also aware of the recent press involvement."

"Given your experience in the field, and DI Tudor's as well as my other colleagues' adulations about your expertise, I'm compelled to trust your judgement in the matter. But I'm also mindful of your past impediments, as well as your current case's tie-in with ours. We are holding her at the Hampshire Constabulary. Please come down here at 8 a.m. sharp."

The distrust was rightful on the officer's part, but despite it, Madison couldn't help but feel giddy at her acquiescence.

She hadn't bothered to take a shower or have breakfast and had hit the road minutes after Palmer's call ended. Pulling up in front of the ageing building of Hampshire Constabulary, she'd spotted Tudor standing on the staircase leading up to the main building.

"She only confirmed her name. We tried showing her the picture of the body and she went into a catatonic state. We haven't got a word out of her since," Tudor informed Madison as they made their way to the interrogation room.

"Where's the boy?" she asked.

"Who?"

She stopped abruptly. "Her nephew, the kid that takes care of the shop with her."

"There were no kids on the premises. Just her. She escaped from the back entrance on our arrival. She tried to hop a fence and ended up breaking her tibia. The officers did a sweep of the shop, but there was no one else there. Quick, let's go before Palmer changes her mind," he said, tugging at her elbow.

She let him guide her towards the room, where they found Officer Palmer.

She offered Madison a nod. "Miss Abbas has given us nothing so far, so I'll let you direct the interrogation. But I don't want you asking questions unrelated to our case."

Madison managed a glum nod in return as they both entered the cold grey room where Afia was settled behind the table. Her hands were cuffed, and she made no attempt to move or even acknowledge their presence. She remained seated, heavily leaning against the back of her chair, staring out at nothing. A few pictures of the St. Elwyn body were spread out in front of her.

Tired would be an understatement - Afia looked utterly *defeated.* A bandage ran across her temple, her face and neck were painted with minor bruising, and her right foot was wrapped in a brace. Her eyes were red and swollen, and clumps of her unkempt hair clung to the dried trails of tears on her face.

Palmer took a seat in one of the two vacant chairs in front of the table and Madison shuffled to the other one.

"Would you like something to drink?" Madison asked when they were settled in.

Afia said nothing. She didn't even look her way or gave any bodily indication of hearing her.

Madison leaned forward, resting her elbows on the table. She needed to appear as approachable as possible if she wanted to draw out a response from the woman.

"I think you know me," Madison said after a long pause. Her voice was even and friendly. "We met a few nights ago... at your shop."

Afia slowly tilted her head to regard Madison with her red, sleepless eyes. Surprise set in them as she recognised her. "You're one of them?"

"Not exactly," Madison replied with a reassuring smile. "You can flip those over," she said, gesturing at the pictures. "If you don't want to look at them."

No response.

Madison collected the pictures from the table and set them aside leaving just one - the least graphic - in front of Afia.

"You're not in any trouble, Afia. I just need you to tell me if you know this woman. You're free to walk if you don't, but you will be wasting crucial time if you do and choose to remain silent. The time that we could've spent determining the reason for her death."

Afia's expressionless eyes remained locked on her restrained hands in front of her.

"I know what you're going through. I've gone through it myself. But this woman," Madison said, tapping the picture, "she deserves more than your silence. Especially now."

Madison watched as Afia's jaw clenched with tension as her lips remained pressed in a line. She still refused to look at the picture, but she seemed much more responsive than she had been only minutes previously.

Madison knew her words were getting through to the woman. Yet, when the words finally left her chapped lips confirming the obvious, Madison felt the hair on her own nape rise.

"She's my sister," Afia said, barely in a whisper. "Sara."

Madison turned to Palmer, who gave her a nod.

She turned back to Afia. "When was the last time you spoke with Sara?" Madison asked.

"Monday."

"Today is a Saturday, so five days ago?"

Afia nodded.

Madison turned to Palmer, who shook her head and silently mouthed, "She doesn't know."

"Did you talk to her on the phone?" Madison asked, feeling a sense of unease settle over her. She didn't want to be the bearer of bad news, and the fact that Palmer was setting her up to be one infuriated her.

"No. We only texted."

"What did you talk about?"

"She told me the same thing she tells me all the time that she misses us. That she'd been meaning to call but couldn't find the right time."

"Who is 'us'?"

"Me and Aron."

"And who is Aron?"

"My nephew,“ Afia muttered.

"The one who tends to the shop with you?"

"Yes."

"Do you know where she was this Monday?"

"At her job in Manchester."

"So, she was not in London?"

"No." Her voice cracked terribly.

"What does she do there?"

"She's a freelancer. She paints murals. She was flown there by her client."

"And when was that?"

"Early October."

"Did she tell you how long it would take?"

"She told me it would take longer than usual."

"And you haven't spoke on the phone since she left? Not even once?"

"No, we didn't… just text. What does that have to do with anything?"

"Did you two usually not talk over the phone?"

"Of course, we did! It was just that this project was taking too much of her time and energy."

"She told you that?"

Afia nodded.

Madison glanced at Palmer, who gave her a curt nod.

"Your sister's body was discovered last week," Palmer informed Afia grimly. She felt Palmer shift in her chair next to her at those words.

Afia's head jerked up. "That's not possible!"

"She's been dead for… over two weeks," Palmer stuttered.

"But we spoke this week!"

"The only probable explanation to that is… the person you were texting… was not her."

Afia's eyes darted around the room as she raked her brain for an explanation.

"So it was her killer?" Afia asked, a crazed look in her tear-stricken eyes.

"It's possible," Palmer informed.

Afia closed her eyes as fresh tears streamed down her face. Disbelief flashed across her face, followed by cold hard dread, as she tried to accept the bleak reality.

Madison reached over to the woman and placed a steady hand on her shaking one.

"Thank you, Afia," Madison offered, knowing full well that her words were falling on deaf ears.

"I need to report this," Palmer declared as she rose to her feet. She pinned Madison with a firm look, "Stay here. I'll return shortly."

And with that she left the room, leaving Madison alone with Afia. She wondered if Palmer was rewarding her for her compliance or simply left for the reason she had stated. Either way, Madison had no intention of letting this opportunity go to waste.

After giving the woman a few moments, Madison asked, "The alley, where we met the other day, is that a common meet-up spot, or is it only exclusive to your business?"

"It's my spot," she replied in a gruff voice. "It's an overall bad area. Only people I deal with come down there since I can't get any business done near the shop."

Madison wondered if that had something to with a certain woman named Nancy.

"Still ended up getting reported, though."

Madison reached for her phone and brought up a picture of Charles on it. "Have you ever seen this person before?"

Afia frowned at the picture. "No. I don't think so."

"He received an email with these coordinates," Madison quickly displayed a picture of the email. "Do you remember sending this out?"

Afia squinted at the screen. "That looks like my address. So, I must've."

"And this is your email address?" Madison asked, zooming into the sender's address on top of the email.

Afia nodded. "He must've sent me a request. Only people who send me requests get the coordinates. I watch them from a distance, and if they look like druggies, they get what they came for. That's my system."

Madison gave her a pointed look. Afia's system clearly wasn't very efficient, but Madison knew better than to take offence at being mistaken for an addict.

"I know it's wrong. But I do it to get by."

"But you're positive you didn't meet this man?" Madison persisted.

"I'm positive. I'm good with faces. I'd remember him."

"Maybe he met with your sister or her son?"

Afia shook her head. "I'm the only one who deals with that type of thing. They're not involved."

"Your nephew certainly seemed very involved to me the last time we spoke."

"He knows what goes on, and I think he's a bit interested, but I try to keep him away from it as much as I can."

"Is there a reason why you do it? Dealing, I mean."

Afia scoffed, despite how miserable she seemed. "If you'd asked me that the last time we met, I'd probably have gotten really defensive. I like to believe that I'm not like other hoppers. That I'm desperate for the money that comes from the trade for all the right reasons. I do it because I need to keep my family going. To ensure that we don't find ourselves on the streets when my sister's out of a job."

"But turns out, once you get a taste of it, you just keep on going. And before I knew it, I had turned into the same kind of people I despised more than life."

Madison observed the pain and the hate that washed over Afia's face. "I think… more than anything else, you despised the fact that your sister's job kept her away from you and her son. Am I wrong?"

Afia's face grimaced as she looked away from Madison. "Was I wrong to hate it? In the end, that's what got her killed."

"We don't know that for sure," Madison offered.

"It's only a matter of time. I mean, she used to take far more jobs before, but ever since we stopped paying our father's medical bills, we could go on much longer with what she earned. And we would've been fine for another year with what little we had saved up from the shop, but I don't know why she was *so adamant* about taking this particular job."

Madison found herself frowning at that. "Well, is your father okay now?"

"I'd like to think so. We got him into this privately funded program called Atomwise last year. They told us that they'd treat him for free. He's doing much better, but you don't really recover from something like Alzheimer's once you have it. And it's especially hard for minorities and immigrants to get proper treatment there."

"Is that so?"

The door behind them unlocked and Palmer stepped in, a cup of a coffee in one hand and a file in the other.

"Can I see my nephew? Before you lock me up?" Afia asked as Palmer returned to her seat.

"Nephew?" Palmer repeated, taking a sip from her cup.

"My nephew! He was inside the store when you people arrested me," Afia stated in a frantic tone. "Please tell me you didn't leave him unattended!"

Palmer shook her head, struggling to swallow the hot liquid, "Our officers did a full sweep after your arrest," she managed while slightly scolding her tongue, "there was no one else in the store."

The horror that flashed through Afia was none like Madison had seen in a while.

15

When Madison left the interrogation room, she blew out the breath she had been holding in her lungs. This was bad for her; she could feel it through the tremors running down her hands. She held them together and looked for a place to sit down, only to be distracted by the sudden unrest around her.

Officers scrambled. Many heading in the direction of the main exit.

"What's wrong?" she asked a nearby officer.

"Somebody tipped off the press," he told her before hurrying off.

She managed to follow him down to the exit and surveyed the loud mob of reporters crowding the steps, being held back by the police.

She knew the case had been publicised, but she had underestimated the extent of it. After all, it was awfully unusual for a single human cadaver to receive that much public attention.

"They think it's a hate crime," someone informed her, answering her mental query. She turned to catch Tudor's displeased face frowning at the crowd. "Or at least, they're trying to pin it as one. I don't think I'm made for interviews."

She offered him a sympathetic smile. "It's all part of the job,

Tudor. Stay strong."

Tudor sighed and turned to her. "You head on home. I'll call you after I'm done with all this nonsense. And since you've pretty much asserted your involvement with the case, I doubt we'll have any more problems with Palmer."

"What do you plan on doing about the kid?"

"There's already a team assigned. Hopefully, we'll find something within the day. Afia will be off to identify her sister, and after that, she'll help us with the investigation. All in all, I have a pretty interesting day ahead. Except for this part," he said, nodding at the awaiting crowd.

Madison sighed, "Well, good luck with that."

"Thanks." She quietly wove her way through the emptier end of the loud mob that, despite the poor weather, shrieked questions and accusations at the desperate officers.

Someone grabbed her by the elbow when she made a run for her car in the open lot. She swiftly turned around and gaped at the man holding her. "Paul?"

"It is you!" he exclaimed, letting go of her arm. "I called your name several times. I was starting to think it wasn't you."

"Do you usually go around grabbing women off the streets then?" she demanded, massaging her hand.

"Sorry," he muttered sheepishly. "Reporter instinct."

"Pretty sure there's nothing like that," she countered but broke into a smile. "What are you doing here?"

"I'm running the story for Channel Three. What about you?"

"I had to meet up with a friend."

"Okay, well," he said, glancing back at the mob. Tudor had emerged from the entryway holding an umbrella to shield himself from the rain, ready to answer questions regarding the investigation. Madison almost pitied the man. These were the more unpleasant instances in their occupation, facing a pack of hungry reporters. "I have to go, but," he turned back to her, "can we meet up soon?"

Madison hesitated. "Sure," she offered, finally.

"Tomorrow evening. I'll call you if that's okay," he told her with an apologetic smile. "It's *so nice* to see you again, Madison."

With that, he took off in the direction of the crowd. Madison made a quick stop at her house to change out of her wet clothes, take a shower, and grab an apple from the fridge. The last thing she needed was an empty stomach getting in the way of her much-awaited quest. After all, Charles had an appointment with a doctor in Kensal Green at midday, and she'd already decided there was no way she could miss it.

***

A sudden bout of sunshine had dispelled all traces of that morning's rain. Finally, a lovely bright, glistening break from the gloomy skies, Madison thought as she drove to Kensal Green. It was a quick eleven-minute drive to Harper's office from Chinatown, and she had almost looked forward to the effortless trip all week.

She parked up and waited.

She checked her watch. It was two minutes to one, which meant Charles would be coming out of the medical complex any minute now.

And he did, alongside Henry. Henry's arm was hooked firmly around Charles', supporting him, as Charles slowly waddled his way toward the parked convertible. Even from a distance it was clear he was having difficulty keeping upright. And the layers of clothing he was wrapped in made it that much harder for him to keep his balance.

Oddly enough, she didn't recall even so much as a gait the last time she'd met him; he had confidently strode his way towards her to heroically reveal his passionate artwork of her. But now, he was having difficulty walking around without support. Something felt wrong.

Maybe he had been lying.

She couldn't deny that there were far too many things off about the man. First off, he was too young to have an illness that primarily affected people over the age of sixty-five, and his brain scans had revealed nothing about it. Secondly, he had founded a small furniture company at the age of twenty that had been defunct for over two decades but had recently received payments from his bank accounts. Payments that had stopped entirely mid-October. These payments, however, were nominal and only amounted to a few thousand when totalled.

A part of her was outraged that she doubted him. She had seen instances of genuine suffering and fear in the man; the kind that couldn't be faked. It was hard to imagine the frail man before her was maneuvering a grand conspiracy all by himself.

But perhaps he wasn't in it alone.

She couldn't jump to conclusions. That's what she kept telling herself.

Taking that extra step to seek out and confirm her theories was her forte. She took pride in being 'extra sure' about things.

She distantly recalled the sweet email Charles had sent her only the previous night. The subtilty of his words and, God forbid, the love in them.

Henry guided Charles into the car; his palm pressed against the top of his head so that it wouldn't hit the roof as he got in. As Madison watched on, she didn't know which part of that scene tugged at her heartstrings.

The car took off, and she set out for the Medical Complex. She chose to avoid the front entrance, instead, she went for the back. A young nurse in blue scrubs and a leather jacket awaited her near the small parking space behind the hospital. He waved at her as soon as he spotted her.

She was led through a narrow back alley and into the building. They climbed a short flight of stairs to the first floor, where the nurse unlocked a weather-beaten door to a windowless room. Large file racks and cabinets filled the average-sized room, and at the centre stood a desk with a computer set-up.

The young man held out his hand expectantly as he shut and locked the door behind them.

She passed him thirty pounds and narrowed her eyes at him when his hand didn't budge. "You know I could go to jail for this," he told her.

Madison rolled her eyes and gave him another twenty.

He led her to the computer and typed in the password.

"You got ten minutes," he informed. "Those," he said, pointing to one of the file trolleys closest to the door, "are the ones for the 12:30 to 13:00 appointments."

She muttered a sarcastic 'thanks' to him as she got to work, distantly hearing the door open and then close.

It took her a few minutes to find the right MD Harper in the facility, and then the patients he had been seeing since searching directly for the name 'Charles Fincher' gave her nothing.

Charles' name was registered under a unique ID code. When she clicked on it, she came upon pages and pages of information about the man. Some of the information dated as far back as 2014.

Harper was a neurologist, and the fact that Charles had been consulting him for more than five years meant that he must have known about his condition much longer than Elizabeth had claimed he did. Or perhaps he was consulting him for a different reason. But a quick look at his records in June 2014 disproved that immediately. Later that month, he would receive the diagnosis, backed by MRI scans and cognitive tests. Scans that showed a loss in brain matter were far from inconclusive.

She took as many pictures as she could of the online files and then went over to the file trolley and found the hard-bound file on Charles. All she found inside that was a small overview and a list of medication and treatments.

According to his family, the overview read:

The subject has shown signs of acute and rapid cognitive decline in the past year. However, the physical examinations offered no convincing indications.

Considering the history of the subject, Cluster B manipulation and pseudodementia could as well be suspected. Still, the visible signs of delirium and other behavioural impairments in him cause us to believe that he is, in fact, in the middle stages of early-onset Dementia.

In the history provided, his family has claimed that he had been showing exceeding signs of apathy, drastic mood changes and societal withdrawal.

For now, moderate cholinesterase inhibitors have been prescribed since the speed of progression has been slow to moderate, but the subject has yet to make a positive reaction to them.

The medicines prescribed to Charles were listed in straight columns followed by their quantities right below the overview. Madison caught sight of the word Donepezil in one of the columns. It was used to treat Alzheimer's, and the thought clenched at her stomach.

Charles' condition was far from a lie. The only thing he had lied about was the true gravity of it.

But why? Why lie about it? Why delay the inevitable?

***

Madison was engaged in vigorous mental sparring when Tudor's call came later that night. It was late, and his voice was groggy and agitated.

"You find anything?" she asked as soon as she picked up.

"Can I ask you something?"

"Sure."

"What exactly is your current case about?"

"Monetary theft. Why?"

"Do you know who Charles Fincher is?" Tudor queried.

"He's a businessman," she answered, feeling unusually prickly at the sudden inquiry.

"According to Afia Abbas, her sister left for the airport for her flight to Manchester on October 3rd. Apparently, her client had arranged for a car to take her to the airport. We checked surveillance footage and can see the car arriving at 'Days of forty-nine'. Sara Abbas gets in the car with her luggage, and it drives off at eleven that night. But the car does not make it to Boundary Street."

"What do you mean?"

"The car vanished somewhere near Cavalier Avenue. The area lacks surveillance, so we're looking into cars with dash-cams that may have been parked near the area that night. But we did manage to run the license plate on Sara's client's SUV, and it belongs to a Charles Fincher."

16

Madison managed to get hold of Gracie's friend's number and called him the next morning. Tyrone Milkovich was a well-spoken man. A biotechnologist settled in New Jersey for a good five years. His parents were close to Gracie's, and the two had practically grown up together. And conveniently, he also worked for Atomwise – which Madison at first thought was a wild coincidence, but was later assured by Gracie that there were a lot of doctors in the US who were serving short tenures at the organisation; mainly because of its advanced science.

"So how exactly do I tell one from the other?" Madison asked as she balanced the phone between her ear and her shoulder while locking the door to her apartment. She'd popped out for a quick groceries run earlier that morning and had to meet up with a contact who had associations with someone who worked at the Bank of Nova Scotia, who had agreed to provide her with whatever information she needed. At the right price, of course.

"By any means necessary," Elizabeth had said, and Madison was determined to do just that.

"Pseudodementia is also a disease of the mind, if not as bad as actual dementia and the big ol' AD," Tyrone Milkovich's heavy voice filled the other end of the line. "But if he has a motive to fake it, then it doesn't fall under either of the two. He is simply tricking people. And if he hasn't been caught yet, he is very good at it, which is rarely ever the case. What I want you to do is look for 'slip-ups'. Every person makes mistakes Miss Sharpe, even the best of us. Pay attention to what he says, to how he behaves, and you'll definitely find something that will give him away."

"I've had the chance to observe him recently, and sometimes he seems… very cheerful, in an almost overly youthful way for his age, and other times he's impassive, indifferent and even violent."

"Bouts of extreme sadness or happiness are not unheard of in Alzheimer's patients. Abusive or violent behaviour can result from overstimulation, confusion, stress, or even in response to abusive behaviour towards them. Alzheimer's aggression is common, and it usually indicates that they're moving on to the later stages of the disease."

"And how long does the end-stage last?"

"One year. Two if he's lucky."

"Oh."

"Yes. After a certain period of time, they can't really be helped. I heard about what happened to Miss Sara. What a tragic ending. I had the chance to speak to her once. She seemed very nice."

"You did?" Madison was taken aback. "When was that?"

"Last year actually. When we flew her family to New Jersey."

"Did she contact you about her father?"

"Quite the opposite, actually. We reached out to needy immigrant families in the UK, and theirs was one of the many we got in touch with. We offered them free treatment and living accommodations, if needed."

"You see, ethnic minorities in the UK - especially immigrants

- lack representation in dementia research. The mental health issues they face are much different from a regular white person, which is why their treatment should differ. But in most cases, these differences are not considered during treatment. And then there's the issue of communal prejudices that some of them face."

"In fact, Sabeer narrowly escaped senicide at the hands of his own family. His daughters got him out of their country and into the UK about two years ago."

Madison eyes widened in shock.

"He's doing well now though," Tyrone continued. "He's reacting very well to the treatments. But I still haven't found the guts to give him the news about his daughter; don't think I ever will. But it needs to be done, sooner or later."

"Are you afraid it'll set back his progress?"

"I'm afraid he'll refuse treatment. He told me that Sara was planning on applying to an art school next year. She was making a portfolio. One of the few things he recalled all by himself in the last few months of his treatment. Abbas was so sure she'd get in. And I have to agree, that girl – she was gifted."

Madison could hear the break in his tone, and she could relate to the sympathy he felt for the family.

"Thank you so much for your time, Dr Milkovich," Madison offered.

"Oh, no worries! Feel free to call me anytime! Any friend of Gracie's is a friend of mine."

Madison dropped the phone in her pocket and ran her fingers through her knotted hair.

From an art prodigy, loving daughter to a corpse in a sinkhole. The world had a funny way of treating the good in it.

She had a visit planned to the Fincher house that day and she wasn't looking forward to it at all. Charles had been the one wanting to see her, and she had reluctantly accepted the offer.

Henry stood on the driveway as he let her car in through the gates. He offered her a nod as he approached her vehicle. "Mr Fincher hasn't been feeling well recently," he informed her through her side window. "I'm afraid he won't be able to entertain you this afternoon."

"Oh, that's really unfortunate," Madison began.

"Let her in, Henry!" Elizabeth called from the front door.

Something flashed across Henry's eyes – annoyance? Anger? Whatever it was vanished from his features just as quickly, leaving behind his cool, unmoved appearance.

He stepped to one side, allowing Madison to get out of her car.

"I've been meaning to call," Elizabeth informed as they entered the living room. "But Charles has been difficult lately. More so than before. Anyway, how far along are you with the case?" She flopped down onto a couch and gestured for Madison to do the same.

"I have several leads," she offered as she sat down on the love seat. "And I'm meeting a contact soon, who has access to records and camera footage. Hopefully, we'll be able to wrap this up pretty quickly."

She had so many questions swirling inside her head that she needed to ask the woman: Where was Charles? Is he okay? Why wouldn't he see me?

But she chose to remain silent under Elizabeth's sharp scrutiny. Elizabeth looked agitated, more so than usual. She wore no makeup other than her bright red lipstick. The satin robe she wore was in wrinkles and scantily thrown-on.

She silently observed Madison. A small smile played at her lips.

"Do you smoke, Miss Sharpe?" Elizabeth asked as she leaned over to the side of the couch to retrieve a box from the table. She pulled out a cigarette and a lighter from it. And it was then that Madison caught sight of the bloodied nail on her right hand.

"No. I don't."

"Hmmm," she said as she blew out the smoke and leaned back against her seat. "Pity, I can't use my nose."

Madison's eyes ran over the thick bandage around Elizabeth's nose as well the bruising under her eyes.

"Charles didn't tell me you were coming here today, and you didn't either, but that's understandable since you have a tendency of showing up announced."

"Pardon?"

Elizabeth scoffed. "I'm saying that on the day you saw my husband crack my nose in two, you were eavesdropping on us. I can't say I really appreciate your prying, Miss Sharpe."

Madison didn't know what to say. She was both enraged and guilt-stricken. After all, she had done exactly what she was being accused of.

"Would you rather have been beaten up then?" Madison asked, narrowing her eyes at the younger woman. "I'm not a doctor, Mrs Fincher but… I don't think that's how you treat someone who's clearly not in their right mind anymore."

"Really? Yet I'm the one who ended up with a broken nose."

"I know what he did was wrong, but he did it because he was provoked, and I think you know that. He showed remorse when he realised what he had done."

Elizabeth turned away from her and drew on her cigarette, letting out a thick cloud of smoke through her gritted teeth, flinching as a small amount of it emerged from her nostrils.

"I know it's hard… especially for you. But you're still with him, putting up with everything, and I don't think a lot of people would be brave enough to do that."

Elizabeth shrugged. "I still love him, despite everything that's happening to him," her voice shook terribly, "to us."

"He still has time left, Elizabeth. Some people with dementia live as long as twenty years after being diagnosed. But he needs to feel loved and to be understood."

Elizabeth's pale blue eyes locked on hers. "You don't understand, Madison," Elizabeth smiled at her. "No one does. But that's okay." She got up from the couch. "He's outside, by the way."

Just as Elizabeth was about to leave she turned around to regard Madison. "Also, don't mind the marks around his neck. He's developed a habit of choking himself recently."

Madison hesitated. She didn't know why. She had doubted her abilities before, but this was the first time she was getting cold feet. The feelings she harboured for Charles were not fair to Elizabeth or even to the man himself, and although she would never let them show, she felt partly responsible for the couple's misery.

Nevertheless, she rose to her feet and slowly made her way towards the French doors leading out to the garden. She found Charles settled on the backless stool, the same way she had seen him on their very first meeting. Voluntarily blocking out the doubt and uncertainty she fostered about the man, she tried to believe that what little she had shared with him was genuine.

But something felt off about him.

He faced a canvas soiled with violent brush strokes. Bright yellow outlines stood out harshly against the placid green ones, forming an ugly, misshapen face. An array of countless half-painted canvases, with equally wild illustrations, were scattered around him.

As she approached him, she noticed that his parted lips were moving, forming audible words that she couldn't make any sense of. The yellow turtleneck sweater he was wearing covered the majority of his neck, leaving only a little reddish lesion on his neck visible. Over it, he wore another knitted V-neck and a brownish cardigan over that.

She took the empty chair next to him and he turned to her as she came within his line of sight, but turned away a moment later; seemingly too focused on his art.

"What are you drawing, Charles?" she asked him.

"Hm?"

"What are you painting today?" she asked him again.

"A face," he mumbled as he dipped his brush in brown paint and proceeded to rub it against the outline of the face.

"Would you like to talk to me for a bit?" she asked him softly.

"Uhm... okay," he muttered. She could sense that he was nervous and jittery, very much unlike his usual self.

"Do you remember that you asked to see me today?"

He looked different. He had lost weight and it showed, even under the layers of sweaters he had donned. Even though it was almost December, the day was warm and pleasant and didn't require as many layers of clothing.

He didn't answer her and instead continued to mumble softly to himself.

"I think he did, until a while ago," Henry informed as he set down a tray of soup and breadsticks on the small table next to the easel. "He brought out an extra chair and even asked me to get you a soft beverage, didn't you, Sir?" he asked, as he leaned over Charles and tucked a paper towel into the neckline of his sweater.

"What happened to him?" she asked quietly.

"It's one of his worse days, I would say. That, and his altercations with Mrs Fincher these past few days have taken a toll on him. I took him to the doctor yesterday, and we were assured that he would be fine as long as he rested. There you go, Sir," he said, gently securing the towel against his employer's chest. He then reached to the tray and brought the bowl to him.

"Did you add rosemary to it?" Charles asked, peering up quizzically at his caregiver.

"Yes, Sir," Henry replied as he fed a spoonful of the soup to his employer, who grimaced after swallowing it.

"It needs more salt," Charles stated as he subsequently returned his attention to his painting.

"Of course, Sir," Henry replied.

"Wait! Don't," Charles said suddenly, "Mum might get mad if she finds out."

Madison looked up at Henry, startled by the statement.

"It's okay. I won't tell her so she won't find out. Would you like some more rosemary to go with it? The mistress says it's good for you."

"Yes, please."

Henry returned shortly afterwards and continued to feed Charles the rest of his soup. He kept asking him open-ended questions about his painting and keeping him engaged in conversation. The latter, however, seemed to have developed a strange enmity with his piece as he slashed at the canvas with thick and uneven brush strokes. The little resemblance the painting initially had to an abstract visage was lost underneath a muddle of wild, violent strokes.

Madison curiously watched the exchange between the two

men. Amazed at Henry's ability at keeping his master engaged and relaxed, and disturbed by Charles' bizarre transformation.

"Sir, I think it's impolite to keep your guest waiting," Henry stated as he set the empty bowl down on the tray. "After all, she came all the way here just to meet you."

Charles shot Madison an awkward glance in response.

"You remember her, don't you?" Henry asked him encouragingly, "It's Miss Anne Murphy. You like to talk to her, so you invited her over."

"I did," Charles mumbled awkwardly, looking down at his paint-covered palms. "I'm hot."

"Would you like to take off your sweater then?" Henry asked him.

"Yes… I-I'll do it in my room." And with that, Charles rose to his feet and walked back inside the house.

"I'm sorry. He's been really anxious lately," Henry informed as he gathered the tray in his hands. "It's important to be patient with him when he's tense."

"But is it okay to lie to him?" she asked.

"It's no use telling him the truth if it confuses him or upsets him, since he'll end up forgetting it again. The least I can do is put him at ease. Make him feel more in control."

Madison discovered a newfound respect for the man in front of her. "You're really good with him."

"My father had suffered - well *lived* with early onset of Alzheimer's as well. While taking care of him, I learned quite a bit. It made me realise where my interests actually lie, and that's how I joined the Domestic Service industry."

"That's nice," Madison said with a smile as she rose to her feet. "I'm glad that you're here for him."

"I appreciate you saying that." Henry smiled back at her, and she realised it was the first time she had ever seen the man do so. But the smile, in itself, was an empty one; offered in an effort to please.

"I'll leave. I don't want to put further stress on him," she said as she started for the doors.

"Would you like me to walk you outside?" Henry asked.

"No, that's alright," she told him and bade him goodbye.

She allowed herself to feel disappointed. After all, that would be the last time she would ever meet Charles. But she also took comfort in the fact that it was all for the best, and she could put to rest the strange way she felt about him and finally move on.

17

"Are you sure?" Tudor asked on the other line.

"Positive. An Audi Q5 was parked in their lot, bearing the same license plate, and it was the only vehicle parked out," she told him, ignoring the clench in her heart.

"Do you really think he is capable of doing something like this? I was made aware that he has been quite ill recently."

"I honestly don't know what he's capable of. Did you find out about the boy yet?"

"I'm just going to let you see it for yourself. I'll forward the footage to you right now."

Madison's laptop dinged, signalling the arrival of an email. She clicked it open to find two video files attached.

"Hang on the line a minute, I'm just going to take a look."

She heaved a sigh and wearily played the first one. The footage appeared to have been taken from a car's dash cam parked near the store. The video was very grainy, but the angle of the camera provided a clear view of the store entrance and the street in front of it.

A minute into the video, a black Audi pulled up in front of the store. A man emerged from the car's driver side, clad in a black suit and a flat cap. His face was illegibly pixelated.

He knocked on the glass entrance of the store and moved away as the door swung open and two women emerged from within the store, hauling suitcases and bags. The driver helped them load their luggage into the car and patiently waited as the two women spoke to each other. A moment later, a third person came out of the store, and one of the two women pulled him into a hug. Pulling away, the woman then leaned forward to hold the latter's face in her palms. They stayed that way for a moment before the woman finally got into the car and the driver followed suit. As the car drove off, the other two remained in their positions for a few more minutes before heading back inside.

"Did you see it?" Tudor asked.

"It's hard to see anything really."

"That's the cleanest we could get it. Does the man's physique look familiar to you? I know it's hard to make out his face, but do you think it could be Charles? You're one of the only few people who's been in contact with him recently."

"I don't know. It's hard to tell. He seems to be about the same height, though. The car looks about the same too. But I didn't catch his hair colour underneath that stupid hat."

She clicked open the second video. This time the camera was positioned a bit farther from the store than before. A man in a black hoodie jogged inside the store. Moments later he came out holding another person against him. The latter sagged heavily against the first man as he was dragged away. She caught a glint of something black underneath the hoodie and, on closer inspection, realised he had worn a beanie underneath the hoodie.

"That's the kid. He took him," she said as she watched the two disappear off-frame.

"We think it's the same guy."

"That's probably the case," Madison remarked, replaying the footage. "Both men make an effort to hide their hair."

"You think that's intentional?"

"Could be. Did you pull any footage from Elwyn?"

"None so far. But we're still looking into it. Also… I think you should know that… we're sending officers to the Finchers' estate tonight to question him. Will that affect your case?"

"Depends. Not like I can stop you, though."

"Not if you want Palmer to hex you. I'll call you later."

Madison sniggered. "Sure."

She stretched out against the wall behind her and steered all her focus to the matter at hand. A moment later, a waiter set down a tray of fish and chips with a side of mushy peas and mint sauce on her table. Madison was their only customer at that hour, and it was deathly quiet around her, despite the hushed conversations among the staff.

After a few mouthfuls, a Vauxhall Corsa pulled up in the diner's marooned parking space. A nervous-looking woman in a brown jacket emerged from the car's driver side, holding a satchel to her chest. Freya, the colleague of Madison's contact, was a junior DPO at the Kensington branch of Scotiabank and had a rather nervous disposition; given away by her incessant posts on an anonymous forum, and the fact that the woman had agreed to meet after a single carefully-worded email from Madison's liaison.

"Would you like some of this?" Madison asked as Freya settled down on the chair across the table.

"I'm good," Freya muttered as she brought out a laptop from its pouch. "How did you find out about me?"

"I saw your posts on the Leeway forum. Let's just say the admin and I are pretty close friends. You were talking about a system crash on the 3rd of October, I believe. One that you were specifically asked to leave out on your report."

The woman flinched as the words left Madison's mouth. "Still, I don't appreciate you threatening me."

"I didn't threaten you."

"You told me that since my husband was having our kids over at his place this week, I would have plenty of time to meet up with you tonight. What did you expect me to think of that?"

"I was being thoughtful. I wanted to catch you only when you were free, but I can see how that might've troubled you."

The woman narrowed her eyes at Madison. "How did you know that me and my husband are separated?"

"*You* told me that, as well as hundreds of other people who regularly view your posts on the forum. You really shouldn't be giving that kind of information away publicly."

"I thought I was anonymous on there!"

"Well, you obviously weren't," Madison asserted with a sympathetic smile. "Did you bring it?"

The woman heaved a sigh as she typed into her laptop and turned it around for Madison to see. A folder of pictures overlooking an empty area with a row of counters.

"The system crash happened at 1:02 p.m. which is lunch hour," the woman informed. "It lasted for five minutes and was limited to the Kensington branch only. These are the pictures from a CCTV camera near a withdrawal counter around 1:01 p.m."

In the row of empty counters, only one was occupied. "I don't know who that is," Freya informed, pointing at the person seated behind the counter. "She is not one of our staff."

"How can you tell?" Madison asked as she craned her neck to make out the pixelated face of the woman seated at the counter.

"We only have two female workers at the branch. Me and our servicing manager, Poppy. Both of us have light blonde hair. This person… doesn't."

"Maybe she's new," Madison suggested, studying the person's long dark hair on the screen.

"We're usually notified when we get new recruits. I don't know who she is."

"What caused the crash?"

"I don't know! I've never seen anything like it before. It could be her because the system went down the very second *she* appeared," Freya sputtered frantically. "I asked my overseer, Martin, about it, and he didn't know anything either! B-but he told me that sometimes these crashes could lead to false positives in the database."

"What kind of false positives?"

"An unauthorised electronic transaction of zero euro to an account in Cayman Islands at around 1:02 p.m. in this case. Bloody specific, isn't it? It had to be Cayman Islands of all places."

"Martin told me to rid the system of it. Which is a load of rubbish and I could tell from his face something wasn't right! And it's common knowledge you're not supposed to delete or alter the transaction history. I didn't even think they were editable until that day. Anyway, he told me not to push the subject any further if I wanted to keep my job. And honestly, I wanted to believe him for a moment because I like my job, and I'd like to keep it. But looking at the CCTV footage from the exact time of the crash - lo and behold - there's an unknown woman tapping away at the counter. I show that to him and the next thing you know, the video file has gone corrupt, and there's nothing to prove my claim anymore!" she let out, all at once, and then stopped to catch her breath.

"Except you knew that would happen and decided to take screenshots. Which is a really smart move."

Freya frowned. "I'm a single mother. I need to be prepared if something happens, and in this case, I need to be able to prove that I'm innocent."

"I assume you deleted the transaction history from the system then?"

"Yes. I had to. Martin made me do it. Whoever was responsible for the crash, I think they're powerful. Like, *really* powerful. Martin seemed to be terrified of them. And he can't lie with a straight face, even with a gun to his head. This wouldn't be the first fraud case in the country, you know."

"You think there's a reason he made *you* do it, don't you?"

"I don't know. But I will do anything to ensure that I'm not the one taking fall for this."

Madison had to give credit where credit was due. The woman in front of her was not only observant but quite quick-witted. She was already planning for a case to prove her unwilling involvement if there was to be a fraud bust in the future, all because her boss had ordered her to do something unusual.

"I know you know something about this. You wouldn't have approached me otherwise," Freya asserted, shooting daggers at her with her deep hazel eyes. "Are you some kind of detective?"

"That I am, and I'm trying to get to the bottom of this. Tell me, Freya, what was the account holder's name for the Cayman Islands account? I noticed that you left that out."

Freya seemed hesitant at first, but she complied and pulled up the information on her laptop.

"Some company named Glasgow Furnishings," Freya offered, promptly turning the screen around for Madison to see.

***

Madison's fingers gripped the knob of her front door as she leaned her forehead against the hardwood for a quiet minute, relishing the sounds of crickets and the unrest from the student residents around her.

"Your boyfriend came looking for you," Jamie's voice startled her.

Madison turned to find Jamie peeking out of her apartment door again, the woman's usual haunt when she was feeling particularly devious against her. Madison's hands itched to wipe off the smug grin on the latter's face. "What?" she groaned out.

"Your boyfriend? The tall blonde guy? He was looking for you, asked me where you were, and I told him I didn't know."

"I don't have a boyfriend, Jamie." She was starting to feel uneasy.

"What do you mean? He told me he was, and he came out of your apartment."

Madison's eyes widened as discomfort rippled through her. She unlocked the door and bolted inside, only to find that it had been turned upside down.

***

"Would you like to stay at my place?" Allison asked, eyeing the sheets laid out on the office room floor. It was the room that Henry had initially assigned Madison when she first started working at the firm, and the one she never had the chance to use since she lived so close to the firm and could do most of her work from home. "The insulation is not the best in this room."

"I'm fine," Madison insisted, sliding into a decade-old sleeping bag that stank horribly of mould, but it would have to do since it was the only one Allison had at hand. She didn't know why she had it in the office, but she was grateful, nevertheless.

"You don't look fine," Allison countered. "You look really pale, and I don't think you should stay alone tonight."

"I'm fine, Allison. Really I am. I just need you to lock up before you go, okay?"

"How long do you even plan on staying here?"

"Just for tonight, I don't think I can go back tonight. But I'll go back tomorrow to get my things and stay at Elwyn for a few days."

"Do you have any idea who he is?" Allison asked. "The psycho who ransacked your place."

"No. I know several 'tall blonde men', but I doubt any of them had anything to do with this. I'll just have to wait until the police have a sketch of the man."

"Makes you glad that you have nosy neighbours for a change, doesn't it?"

Madison chuckled. "I suppose."

She caught Allison frowning at her again. "I'm fine, go on. I'll call you if I need anything," Madison assured. Allison looked far from convinced, but gave her a nod regardless and left. A minute later, Madison heard the lock from the main entrance slip in place. She palmed the spare key she had been handed a while ago and slowly brought out her hands from underneath the layers of the sleeping bag. They were sweaty but cold at the same time.

The only thing she had with her was her laptop and her phone. She had made the right decision to have taken her laptop out with her that day. A rare feat that had saved her a lot of trouble.

But what unnerved her most was that the intruder hadn't been looking for anything in particular, as given away by the randomly broken furniture in her apartment. None of her locked drawers had been tampered with, and even the duffel bag she had stuffed underneath her bed had remained untouched. Nothing but her peace of mind had been taken away.

Perhaps it was a warning to her. It wouldn't be the first time somebody had attempted to vandalise her home in order to ward her off a case. It would, however, be the first time someone had successfully broken in. But back then, she was gallant and young. She had been desensitised to aggression and such random acts of hostility. Now, however, she was a coward.

All she could think about at that moment was if he had found her, what would he have done to her?

She hoped that it was, after all, the shadow of a fear she had once experienced. She didn't have anything to lose anymore.

She scoffed, looking down at her shaking palms that seemingly disagreed with that sentiment of hers. She was truly, genuinely terrified. It all had fallen in place the second Jamie had mentioned that the intruder was a blonde man. But what bothered her the most was the fact that a part of her already knew that she was being pursued, and she had chosen to willfully ignore all signs of it happening. The uneasy feeling of being watched in Elwyn on the last day of her downtime, the figure standing by the tree line later that same day, it all came flooding back to her. He had been there that day, and now he's been in her home.

An odd thought crossed her mind; one that disturbed her deeply. Her pursuer had been in Elwyn around the same time Sara had been killed. Although there was no evidence that she had been killed in Elwyn itself, the timing felt strangely suspicious.

Madison grabbed for her phone to dial Tudor and wasn't surprised to find a few missed calls from him, as well as several from Paul. She distantly recalled Paul's invitation from the previous day and felt oddly guilty at the fact that she had forgotten all about it.

She tried calling Tudor but his phone was switched off. She sent him a text asking him to call her ASAP. Then, her finger hovered over the missed calls from Paul.

"Where are you?" she asked as soon as he picked up.

The last thing she wanted was to be alone.

18

"Now to report on the St. Elwyn slaying. An alleged kidnapping has been reported in association with the slaying. A fifteen-year-old boy named Aron Abbas was taken from his home-"

"Can you turn that down please?" Paul asked the bartender, who complied with a nod. But Madison's eyes refused to leave the screen as she watched the footage of the boy being carried out and away, while the police gave chase to his aunt on the other end of the frame.

Palmer had decided that releasing the video to the press would encourage witnesses to come forward, since law enforcement had almost no leads as to who the man in the hoodie was or if he was, in any way, connected to the slaying.

He was a rather tall man, Madison noticed with a frown.

A soft nudge to her shoulder finally broke her out of her thoughts. She turned to face Paul Jennings sat on the seat next to hers.

"I've been trying to get your attention for a while now," he said with a guilty grin. "You okay?"

"Yeah, sorry, I just have a lot of things on my mind, that's all," she drawled. "I'm okay. What about you? How's work?"

"Tiring," he heaved. "But it's good to be back. Hopefully, I'll be in Westminster for a while."

"That's good," she trailed off. She couldn't quite explain the sudden awkwardness she felt when being close to him, since they had both spent a good portion of their lives together. She wondered if she should shift the topic to the Finchers' case, but thought against it immediately after.

An untouched martini sat on the table in front of her. It had been there before she had arrived, and she resisted the urge to take a sip from it.

"I'm sorry I haven't called in a while," he muttered with a tragic smile. "It's been hard," he added, lightly nodding to himself.

Madison tiredly rubbed at both eyes.

"My girlfriend broke up with me," he added chuckling, as the bartender placed a pint of beer in front of him.

And my house was broken into.

"Wait, Rebecca? You two were inseparable," Madison joked with a grin. "How long were you together? Six, seven months?"

"Four and a half," he corrected as he took a swig of his drink. "I thought so too, until she emptied an entire bottle of Vermouth on my head and stormed off. It was vintage too, which is a pity," he drawled with a sad smile.

He looked good, Madison noted. But then again, he always had. His dark hair was longer, almost reaching his shoulders. He was clean-shaven, but the dark lines that ran along his hazel eyes made him appear rugged and rakish regardless. The sleeves of his black jacket stiffened gracefully at his biceps and were clear to see in the dimly lit pub. Some of the girls in the adjoining booth leered at him openly, but he took no notice as he held Madison's gaze with an almost impish glint in his eyes that would've made her legs go weak all those years ago.

The gentle, sheepish man that she had fallen for so many years ago was nowhere to be seen. Her heart clenched painfully at the realisation of how much they had both changed.

"That is so like you," she said, shaking her head. She turned away and stared down at her drink.

"Told me that I didn't love her as much," he said, shaking his head.

"Well, did you?"

"You and I both know that things don't work that way for the two of us anymore," he offered fondly.

Madison nodded. He was right. The few relationships – if you could call them that – she'd had after Paul were short-lived and often ended badly. Love was non-existent and had become something of a privilege that they could no longer partake in.

"Well, she wasn't wrong," he added.

Madison smiled as she tapped her finger against her glass in anticipation of the trap he made a habit of setting for her in the few times they had met up after their separation.

She could feel him staring at her. She turned to face him with a smile, but her gaze switched to the group of girls seated on the booth behind Paul. They seemed unabashed by his lack of interest in them, and one even got up and made her way towards him.

Madison's hand shifted and placed it on top of his possessively. His eyes glistened eagerly at the contact, but he said nothing. Just a ghost of a smile played at his lips as he peered at her curiously, drawing the words out of her mouth. Perhaps she wouldn't need him to set his trap!

"Let's get out of here," she whispered to him.

***

She woke up with a splitting headache. The sheets slipped aside as she pulled herself up to lean against the headboard of the bed. Besides her, Paul pulled the covers over his face as he shimmied further down the bed.

The room was painfully bright as the morning light seeped in through the half-open blinds of the window. She had spent the night at Paul's.

The vibration of her phone on the floor caught her attention. Reaching for it, she cursed the number of missed calls from Tudor. Just as she was about to dial the number, his call came up again.

She climbed out of bed and barely registered the oversized t-shirt she was clad in. It was one of hers. Paul had kept the things that she hadn't taken with her after their divorce. She was surprised by the amount of clothes that were still stashed somewhere in his massive closet. The smell of fabric softener on the shirt made it painfully obvious that he had washed it recently.

"Hey," she said into the phone.

"Oh, thank God!" Tudor panted on the other line. "Why weren't you picking up?"

"I had a late night. Why? What's wrong?" Madison asked.

"Charles Fincher is missing," Tudor said frantically.

Madison's eyes widened. "What do you mean?"

"He's gone. We went to his house last night and his wife told us that he'd been gone all day. Have you heard from him recently?"

"No," Madison sputtered as she tried to wrap her head around the news. "The last I saw him was on Saturday. It was obvious that he was out of sorts, so we didn't get to speak much."

"Palmer thinks there's a good chance he's our man. He might be the slayer."

"Really! Does she have any proof yet?"

"Other than the fact that Sara Abbas was last seen getting into his car and that he has conveniently decided to disappear right after we release the footage of the kidnapping."

"But the man's face isn't actually visible in the footage, and there's a good chance that his vehicle had been used without his permission. Maybe it was someone who had access to it. I'm telling you, Tudor, given the condition he is in, he isn't capable of-"

"Charles was away from home the first week of October. He didn't tell Elizabeth where he went, but she assumed he had gone on vacation. We checked and they were supposed to be visiting the Pamukkale Hot Springs in Turkey, but Charles had called and cancelled a week before their planned departure. No one knows where he was that week or what he was up to."

"We've been able to get a warrant. We'll be searching his house today. And... I need you to stay away from the family from now on."

"That's..." What more could she tell him? That she couldn't do that because she was in the middle of a case that involved him when she herself had sworn that she wouldn't go near Charles again? That seeing him does her more harm than good?

"Okay. But Tudor, I really don't think he did it."

"I will take that into account. But if he contacts you, you need to let me know immediately."

She doubted he would. He probably didn't even know who she was. "I will."

A sense of panic filled her as soon as she hung up.

She found her laptop in the bag by the door where she had left it the previous night. A quick search on the internet informed her that the news about Charles being suspected of the St. Elwyn murder had yet to break. She knew her relief was short-lived, and she could do little about that. She brought up the screenshots from the footage of Aron's kidnapping and paused it as soon as the hooded man came into frame. Focusing on the zoomed in, enlarged pixels of the man's side profile, something lingered at the back of her mind but she couldn't put her finger on it.

The hoodie seemed somewhat familiar. A rather long one that reached his knees and had long slits cut on the sides. It wasn't an uncommon design, but she was sure she had seen the same one recently.

Paul's house was a mess, but it was big enough to seem spacey; despite the mounds of washed laundry and stacks of books piling up. Paul had been very particular about the kind of house that would be suitable for a family of three when he had bought it around ten years before.

Three bedrooms and an extra one for guests. An ample home for the family that they had once planned to build together. A gift to her from him a year after their marriage, a few months after she had broken the news about her pregnancy to him. They were both in their early twenties. She was a nervous university student, and he was a rookie writer for a local news channel when they welcomed their first child. That was enough reason for Paul to spend all his life savings on the house. And although she had demanded that they wait until they were more settled in life to buy a property, she had ended up admitting defeat to his pleading eyes. Back then, he was a bashful lanky young man, an overbearing optimist who wore nothing but brightly coloured polo shirts and track pants and who had made her feel like the happiest person alive.

She swallowed a knot that had risen in her throat as she

brought down the kettle from one of the shelves. As she waited for it to boil, she pranced about in the living room, gathering clothes that they had discarded the night before and stuffed them down into a laundry basket by the washer. The counter next to the machine held a wild assortment of books, all strewn untidily on the stone countertop.

The title of one of the books caught her attention and she unconsciously picked it up.

"I see you made coffee." Paul stood, leaning against the door frame. "And that you've found my books."

"Nanotechnology?" she asked as she held up the metallic blue book for him to see.

"Yeah, it's something I've been interested in lately."

She hummed as she gazed at the rest of the books.

"What?" he asked.

"Gracie told me she met you at a seminar back in Philly." Madison put the book down.

"Yeah. She did. I kind of went all around the country this past year," he drawled with a smile as he moved toward the small tea table that stood in front of a full-length window in the kitchen. "My team and I were working on this documentary on American war veterans. Pretty interesting stuff," he said, nodding to himself.

Madison poured the coffee into mugs and brought them over to the table, where she flopped down on a chair next to Paul. "Tell me more," she urged pushing a cup towards Paul.

Pressing the cup to his lips he smiled, "Well, he is turning seventy-seven this month. He served in the military for over thirty years. Enlisted at around seventeen, I think. A looker back in the day. Probably twice my size at my age and all muscle," he drawled with a dry chuckle. "He married the love of his life, had three beautiful kids, and they all adore him. Then sadly, tragedy struck. He started forgetting basic things at first, but it gradually worsened in his late sixties, and now he doesn't even recognise himself."

"Dementia?" she asked.

"Yeah. Alzheimer's. It was horrible watching a man like him slowly fall apart. It makes you wonder what'll happen to us in the next thirty years or so," Paul offered with a frown. He was disturbed by the thought.

"Well, we still have time," she offered, reaching out to press her palm against Paul's. "It must've been hard for you to see that."

Paul smiled sadly. "He was a hero who protected his country, his family," he lamented. "What's the point of it all, right? If you'll just suffer at the end?"

Madison unconsciously squeezed his hand at the bitterness in his words.

"His daughter, she asked me if I could reach out to people who were working on potential cures for Alzheimer's and other degenerative diseases. My crew and I spent three and a half months with his family, and we've grown really fond of them. They're good people," he said affectionately. "We reached out. To a lot of people, in fact, and Gracie's friend was one of them and the one we stuck with in the end."

"Nanotechnology to cure dementia?" she asked.

Paul nodded. "Milkovich's arguments were convincing. He works for a nonprofit organisation called Atomwise. I think it's been over five years since they came into being. But it's only recently that they're taking in patients. Given the relative newness of his organisation, Riley's family was initially hesitant. Still, we got him to attend a few of the programs with Doctor

Milkovich's team back in June last year."

Madison perked up at the mention of the organisation's name. "I think I've heard about them. Do their treatments work?"

"It did actually, to an extent. But Riley passed away in January before they could make any noteworthy observations, aside from his recovering memory. The doctors warned us that making a full recovery was close to impossible due to his age. But I still remember the shine in old Riley's eyes when he called me by my name the last time we met. He was grinning like he knew that would surprise me. It was incredible. This whole thing with him was actually what got me into the subject."

"And it had me thinking, you know? Life is so precious and short, and we've got to live it to the fullest because this is all we have, all we will ever have," his head was shaking from side to side. "I think Livi would want that for us too," he added almost in a whisper.

"I don't know how to do that. A part of me died with her, Paul. And I know it's the same for you too. It took me so long to get back on my feet again, to go out and get myself out of my head. And quite honestly, I don't think it gets any better than this," she said, peering up at him. "Not without her."

Paul gazed down at their fingers. "Come back to me, Madison," he mumbled quietly. "We are good for one another. We will get better, stronger even, if we are together."

"Don't, Paul. I can't. I couldn't two years ago, and I can't now." The throbbing in her head worsened and she pulled her hand away from his.

"Just listen to me," he pleaded, his eyes finding hers. "Just... we don't have to get together, not now, not unless you want to. Just move back in with me—this house is as much yours as it is mine. I still have all of your things. Let's get through this together," he said softly.

"I can't."

"I know you still get nightmares. I do too. And I know you need me, as much as I need you," he drawled. "Please. Tell me you'll think about it."

She pursed her lips. Paul knew how her mind worked; he knew exactly what to say and when to say it in order to make her accede. She was almost sure that he did it on purpose, and for the most part, it was effective.

19

Holding a box of case files tightly to her chest, Madison strode down the small set of stairs of her apartment to the walkway where Paul's car was parked. With her eyes nearly closed, to protect them from the strong wind, she dumped the box and the rest of her belongings in the trunk. She was moving back in with Paul for a while. A part of her had been wary about how easily she had given in to him.

Paul was still in Madison's apartment sealing boxes and gathering the rest of her needful things. He had realised they would need more packing boxes and sent her to the shops while he packed.

She almost cringed at his eagerness to have her move in with him when deep down she knew it would never work between them. The few nights they had shared together had been a temporary escape, and it could be nothing more. But she needed a place to stay until her 'stalker' situation was over, so she was ready to take whatever offers she had available to her; Paul being the most convenient.

As she walked down to the store across the street, the grim weather did little to discourage the people who sought to spend their weekends outside. Just as the traffic lights turned red and the cars came to a halt, heavy rain started to fall down hard. Her breath caught sharply as the cold drops of water ran over her skin. People around her ran to take shelter. In the flurry of movement around her, she caught sight of a man standing on the other side of the crossing. He stood unmoved in the rain and stared blankly at the greyish pavement on which he stood. The grey turtleneck shirt that he wore was stained and tattered at the ends.

As if sensing her eyes on him, he slowly looked up, and his gaze locked onto hers.

As the lights turned green, she moved. Cars honked at her, and a few obscenities were directed her way, but she paid them no heed as her feet unwittingly carried her towards him.

"Charles?" she called as soon as she reached him. "What are you doing here?"

"I know you," he whispered, almost as if to reassure himself.

Madison reached out to place a careful hand on his shoulder. "Are you okay?"

"I know who you are. Please, please take me home?," he asked jerkily as he shook underneath Madison's hand. He looked down at his feet and pulled his palms into fists at his side as a tear slipped down his bloodshot eyes. "I want to go home."

"Who did this to you?" she asked, tightening her hold on his shoulders. "Charles?"

***

"I think we should call the police," Paul suggested as he paced Madison's living room.

"We can't. Not yet," Madison asserted, as she knelt on the floor in front of Charles who was settled on the couch under several layers of blankets. He was still drenched to the bone.

They both were, but Paul had unreasonably refused to let him change or move around until he was offered a proper explanation.

"Who the hell is this man?" Paul stopped his pacing to leer pointedly at the other man.

At that, Madison hauled her ex-husband back into the bedroom by his elbow. "He's Charles Fincher," she said as soon as they weren't within Charles' earshot. "I don't know how he found me, but he's here… somehow," she said impatiently. The cold from her wet clothes was seeping into her skin, making her shudder.

"Wait. Charles Fincher? From Fincher Corporations?"

She nodded helplessly.

"Well, why can't he remember his own name then?"

"He has moderate dementia. But I think he remembers me."

"Did you give him your address?" Paul heaved exasperatedly.

"No! I seriously don't have a clue how he found me," she asserted, shaking her head.

"Did you see those cuts on his arms? Those are knife wounds, Madison! This is clearly not something we can deal with by ourselves!"

"I know! Don't you think I know that? I just don't think it's safe," Madison hissed. "For him!"

"How is he not safe? Why are you acting this way?" he demanded.

"Look, I can't tell you everything, all right? But I need you to stay calm. If we panic, he panics. I just can't take him to the police yet, or send him home until I know who did this to him." Madison glanced at her guest's tall form hunched over in her living room. "He needs our help, Paul."

"But this isn't your problem, Maddie! You can't keep doing

this, jeopardising your life for the sake of strangers! It hurt you before, and it'll hurt you again!" Paul yelled as he raked his fingers through his hair.

"Look at him!" She pointed at the darkened stains on Charles' shirt, right above his waist bone. "Those are bloodstains, Paul!" she said through gritted teeth as she glared at Paul. "I'm not turning him away, not now. I'll do this alone if I have to."

"What are you even-,"

"Look, go back home," she said, cutting him off, "bring him a change of clothes. Then we can figure this out. Please, Paul. I need you to do this for me."

Paul pursed his lips, staring at the other man from a distance and then shot out of the room.

"Charles?" she called gently as soon as the front door slammed shut. She knelt on the floor in front of him and inspected the purple wounds staining his face. "Do you remember what happened? Who did this to you?"

"I would like to go home," Charles asserted nervously as he frantically scratched at his palm. "Take me home."

The movement distracted Madison, and she reached for his hand only to have it slapped away. For a moment, she was stunned. She studied the man before her; it was evident he was scared. Although he didn't recall what had happened to him - his brain having willfully forgotten those distress-filled moments to enable his mind to cope - there was still the shadow of fear weighing down on him.

She needed to tread cautiously.

"I'll take you home in a bit, but let me fix you up first, okay?"

Charles' eyes still refused to meet hers.

"You're safe now," she assured him. "No one can hurt you here."

After a moment of hesitation she asked, "Can I see your hand? I just want to check if you're hurt."

Charles didn't move. Madison slowly reached for his hand again and this time he let her touch him. She carefully retrieved his hand and opened up his palm. There appeared to be letters and numbers under angry scratch marks. Whatever Charles had used to write had been dug into his skin deeper than necessary, to the point that some of the letters were swollen and bleeding.

The letters citing her own name and the numbers of her street. That explained how he had found her.

"Did you write this, Charles?" she asked, trying to suppress the strain in her voice as she gaped at the writing across his palm.

But he must've sensed her alarm since he recoiled from her touch and freed himself from her hold.

She didn't retract her hand, though. Instead, she gently reached over again and pulled his shirt up until the gnarly knife wound on his waist came into view. He flinched but thankfully allowed the contact.

"This could get infected. Are you hurt anywhere else?" she inquired, eyeing the brown clumps of dried blood clinging onto his unwashed, broken skin with a grimace. Fortunately, the wound didn't seem too deep.

"No."

"Are you sure?"

He closed his eyes. She knew he wasn't.

"Why don't I run you a nice warm bath, and we can talk about this later?" she suggested in a soft voice, one that she often used with Livi when she was sad.

"Take me home," he asserted yet again.

"I promise you I will."

"The kid," he mumbled. "He's there all alone."

"What kid?"

"I don't - I don't know."

"Tell me when it comes to you, okay?"

Charles nodded and looked away.

Paul returned an hour later with a bag of clothes that he dumped in Madison's spare room.

"He's not wearing anything under there, is he?" Paul inquired, shooting a disapproving glance at Charles, who was wrapped up in a freshly washed duvet. She had managed to clean and patch up most of his wounds, but the puncture on his waist needed stitching, and she wasn't well-versed with that. She had instead cleaned it and bandaged it for the time being. Charles had been surprisingly calm during the whole ordeal, but she didn't want to test his patience any further than necessary.

"His clothes are soaked through," she offered as Paul clomped his way to the kitchen. "The wound on his waist is not that deep, but it still needs stitching."

"You're really trying to milk my nursing degree, aren't you?" he asked.

Madison smiled and gestured to one of the cupboards in her kitchen. "There's a first aid kit in there."

She was thankful to have him around. In his worst moments, Paul was disagreeable and unreasonable, but he was still willing to help if she ever needed him. She cherished that part of their relationship.

Madison dusted and aired out her spare bedroom, while Paul had stitched up the other man and aided him in the shower.

An hour later, Charles was perched on top of the single bed in Madison's spare room, nervously rubbing at his neck. The choke marks stood bright against the pale skin of his neck.

"Get into these," Paul offered, placing a t-shirt and a pair of pyjama pants on the edge of the bed.

"So, what do we do now?" Paul asked as he walked back into the living room, making sure to close the guest room door on his way out. "The guy was obviously attacked."

"Did you see the…?" she asked, gesturing at her neck.

Paul nodded grimly.

"He had them the last time I went to their house."

"What? Why didn't you report it?" he demanded as he flopped down on the couch next to her.

"I don't know. I had my doubts. His wife told me he did it to himself. And I just didn't think it was any of my business," she tried.

"Well, you certainly don't think that way anymore!" Paul spat as he pulled at his hair. "For all we know, it's the wife that did this to him."

Madison froze at those words. She gaped at Paul, who seemed taken aback by her reaction.

"You don't think?"

"I don't know. I don't think so. The police were at his place last night. I'm sure they checked with the house staff as well. Elizabeth was already notified about the visit the day before, so I doubt she'd do something this reckless. And those cuts on him are fairly recent."

"Have you called her?"

"No. I was about to, but it doesn't seem like a good idea anymore."

"Yeah."

"Oh god," she breathed out. "What time is it?" she asked, sitting up to check her watch.

19:08 p.m. She had about thirty minutes before her agency closed for the day. "I need to go. Can you look after him?"

"Where are you going?" he frowned, following her into the bedroom.

"I need to look into a few things." She pulled on a hoodie and a pair of track pants. "Just don't let anyone in until I'm back, okay?" she added as she grabbed her keys and her bag.

"Okay. Just be back soon," he called to her as she closed the door and jogged out into the cold night towards her car.

20

"But what if she is home?"

"I'm sure she won't be there," Madison asserted.

"But what if she *is*?" Allison argued.

"Look, please just do what I asked you to do. I already texted you the information of the broker's number. I'll call you back in an hour."

She rang the buzzer next to the gate and was immediately let in. The front door cracked open as she parked her car, and Henry emerged from it.

"Miss Sharpe," he said, "I'm afraid no one's home at the moment."

"Oh, uh, do you mind if I still come in?" she asked. "I'd like to speak with you if that's okay."

Henry was taken aback by the request. "Of course," he said, breaking into a smile. "Come on in."

She wove her way to the living room that looked far darker than usual.

"I'm sorry if it's too dark. With the master and the mistress of the house gone, I only like to keep on what I need."

"Oh, no. It's fine," Madison assured.

"I suppose I can't get you anything since you don't eat outside food."

He smiled at Madison's shock at those words. "Kind of hard not to notice," he said. "What can I help you with… Miss Sharpe?"

It wasn't something that she had been trying to hide, and it was obvious for Henry, of all people, to have noticed it. But something didn't sit well with her. Something had bothered her the second she had stepped foot inside the house. And it had little to do with the smiles being passed her way.

But at least this time, Henry's elation seemed oddly genuine.

"Was Charles home last night?" she asked.

"I'm afraid he wasn't."

"Do you know where he was?"

"I don't know."

The challenge in his eye betrayed his words. He was lying.

And that alone confirmed what she had suspected about the man.

"Miss Sharpe, has anyone ever told you that you're extremely gifted at reading people?" Henry sneered.

"Where was he, Henry?" she asked again, her hand slipping into the bag at her side.

"Serving his purpose. Which he obviously failed since you're here," he added with a smile.

In a split second he rose to his feet and shot towards Madison, her hand slammed square on his stomach. The taser jittered against her grip as it transferred a hefty amount of voltage into her attacker.

Henry's groans ripped through the quiet house as he fell to his knees, his hands floundering for the support over her.

But before she could push him away, she registered, too late, the sting of a syringe against the side of her neck. She gritted her teeth as she was drawn into the darkness.

As she regained consciousness, Madison doubled over and couldn't stop herself from vomiting. When the adrenaline from that exertion had finally died down, she risked losing consciousness again. She bit the inside of her cheek until she tasted blood, hoping the sting would keep her from slipping.

She couldn't feel much of her body, aside from a dull ache at the side of her head.

Looking around, she saw nothing in the pitch black and momentarily panicked, until her eyes adjusted to the darkness around her. She eventually made out soft shadows from distant objects and realised the room was one she was strangely familiar with.

She was sat on a chair that appeared to be bolted into the floor. Her hands were tied behind her back, but her feet were free. She attempted to kick them around, and her right foot knocked against something hard and flat. She leaned her head forward, as far as the chair would let her, but her forehead thumped against a cold hard glass surface.

A panicked breath escaped her dry mouth when she eventually realised where she was.

As if on cue, Charles' office room door flung open. Blinding lights washed over her. She squirmed and shut her eyes against the sudden brightness. Her hands attempted to break free to shield them.

"Is that too bright?" a voice asked her. "I can lower it a bit. Actually, I think I'll just leave it as it is for now. Consider it your punishment, aside from the number I did on you. I don't shy away from anger issues, you see. But I only hurt you a bit, so hopefully, you won't be concussed for too long."

She squinted at her captor who was smiling down at her from the other side of the glass. "Oh, now that I think about it, Sara hated these lights as well."

"Did you kill her?" Madison asked flinching at how weak and broken her voice sounded.

"She killed herself. I did coerce her a bit, but that's all I did. It was her sister's drugs that killed her, actually. She prices them quite high, but they're surprisingly well cut."

"Where's Elizabeth?" she managed to sputter through her sore throat. "Did you kill her too?"

"Oh, no. I wouldn't do that to that… gnat. That's an appropriate term for her, no? Well, she and I kind of have a pact, so I'm not really allowed to touch her. As for where she is, she's gone. She got what she needed from you."

"What?" Disbelief flashed through her. After a brief silence she realised what he meant."

"The furniture company was the key that you, albeit unintentionally, handed to her. She's capable of doing her own digging, you know. You shouldn't seem so surprised. You never trusted her in the first place. You deliberately overlooked everything about her because her marriage was falling apart. But trust me when I say this - she's the only one responsible for it."

"You know, she was picked off from the streets by Hedrick. An orphan with no immediate family. She grew up at the house and was engaged to Charles when she turned eighteen. But when Hedrick died, she refused to marry him. She wanted to live her life, so she did. And then out of the blue, she showed up two years ago and tells him that she's ready. I wonder what changed her mind."

"What did I do then? Why am I here?"

"You're here because you came to me. Although, I did send Charles your way, hoping you'd take the hint and stay away, but you didn't. Now tell me, how'd you find out about me? What gave it away?"

Madison remained neutral at the inquiry, even though her body ached and screamed for her to attack the man in front of her.

"The hoodie," she answered. "The one you wore when you took Aron. I remember seeing it in Charles' closet."

"That can't be the only reason."

"I guess like most men in the Fincher family your father was affected by young-onset, familial Alzheimer's – a rarer type of dementia which has a strong genetic link. Hedrick's brother was affected by it. And now, your cousin, Charles, has it."

Henry's smile widened. "That's quite spot on, I must say." His eyes lingered on her a moment longer than she was comfortable with. "You're not going to ask me about the kid?"

"I have a feeling you won't tell me the truth. So, no."

Henry looked taken aback by her words and broke into a fit of uncontrollable laughter.

"You never cease to amaze me, Madison," he sputtered as he struggled to catch his breath. "But… what if I told you I did to him exactly what the ring had done to your daughter."

She stopped dead at those words.

"Shut up," she muttered over the sound of her rapidly beating heart.

Henry reached over to place a hand against the glass.

"The police will find his disfigured body in the park, near your husband's house. And I'll make it so that it'll all be your fault, just like it was with your daughter."

"No… no…," she stuttered, blinking back tears.

"How were you even allowed to work the case when the victim was your own daughter? I know the media didn't cover the case as much as you'd expect them to, but there was almost no mention of it anywhere for a few months. Was it your skills that kept you in the case or was it your connections?" he asked. "I wonder, is that why you resigned from the force, Madison?"

"Did you know that my father burned to death? Intentionally set on fire by Hedrick's men."

Madison's eyes widened in shock.

"What?"

"It was covered up, of course, so I'm not surprised you didn't know. Hedrick took care of him a year after he inherited the corporation. He couldn't even wait until the disease finished him off. But unlike you, I couldn't do anything about it."

"Is that why you're killing them off? Revenge. For your father?"

"I wouldn't call it revenge. I associate that term with a lot of anger and desperation. I am merely out to purge the Fincher bloodline."

"My father was weak, and he had it coming either way, as does Charles."

"All those deaths…"

"That's right. I caused them. I had to get rid of them before they branched out and had families. It was, of course, hard to make them all appear 'natural', but I had years to plan ahead."

"Charles though, he's weak like my father. I won't need to waste my efforts on him."

"Then why are you here?"

"To watch over him, in a way. And he repays me back by being my confidant."

"You have a way of treating your confidants."

"I punished him for invading my privacy. As simple as that," he admitted with a smile. "He even accompanied me to Lyndhurst that day. I made him watch when I hit her in the head and told her I'd keep hitting her if she didn't bite her wrists off. She was high. She probably didn't feel a thing when she bit into her veins. When I turned back to him, he was foaming at the mouth! Okay, now that we're all up to date, do you have any more questions?"

"What did you make her do? You held her captive for over a month. What did you do to her in that time?"

"That is a question for a different time. But you could look through all the paintings in there. Maybe she's left clues for you to find. I'll bring you some food in the meantime."

And with that, he took his leave.

She rotated her wrists back and forth in an effort to loosen the rope binding her hands. Its rough surface dug into her skin, causing burns, and she grit her teeth against the pain. The effects of whatever Henry had given her was already wearing off little by little, and she could feel the pain all around her body growing sharper - to the point that she was desensitised to it.

By the time the rope slipped off her wrists, the skin around them was broken and sore. Madison attempted to stand up, but her legs gave way as soon as she did. Defeated, she flopped back down on the chair.

She patted her pockets and wasn't surprised to find that they had been emptied.

She squinted up at the glass walls that were keeping her encaged and noticed that the scratch marks along it looked far more prominent from her side of the glass. Sara certainly hadn't gone down without a fight against the man, and the thought pleased her. But the glass was thick, and no amount of barehanded pounding would cause it to break. A small glass door with hinges fitted at the corners served as the only entrance into the glass chamber. It was locked, of course, but she still attempted to push it open at least once. She checked the hinges and noticed a brownish stain on them. She scraped the brown bits with her nails and realised that it was dried blood; underneath, the steel looked new and unscathed.

Madison leaned back against a leg of the chair and studied her surroundings yet again. Stacks of half-filled canvases and complete paintings – ones she had already seen during her first time in the room. On closer inspection, she saw that almost all of the paintings were rough copies of one another. They all depicted a small bridge over a weed-filled pond.

She recognised the short brush strokes and the almost life-like depiction of light against the objects in the scene.

"I had Sara practice quite a lot."

Madison jumped at the sudden intrusion. She turned to find Henry leaning his forehead against the glass. He held a food tray against him and smiled at her surprise. Thankfully he hadn't noticied that Madison's hands were untied.

"She was great, but I needed her to be perfect," he explained as he walked around the chamber and to the small door.

"Perfect for what?"

"I won't be answering that just yet. You know, Hedrick had this built to house his taxidermy tiger. He hunted it and stuffed it himself. It was a grotesque thing to look at and gave me nightmares when I first came to this house. Charles took it down after Hedrick died and decided to grow a small indoor garden in it. Thus, the lights. But sadly, nothing ever grew. That's just what the Finchers' bloodline does. It plunders and poisons."

"That said, Charles didn't remove the vacuum function needed to conserve a badly done taxidermy animal. So, if you don't listen to me, I will make it so that you can't breathe in there. Go on now. Scurry off to the corner. I can't have you running away yet."

Madison retreated to the corner farthest from the door. She watched as Henry used a key to unlock the small lock and waited until the door was pushed open. As soon as he slid the tray in, she lunged forward and pushed the tray against the hinge of the door, sticking it in between the bottom of the door and the sill.

As Henry frantically reached inside to pull at the tray, she grabbed his hand and used her weight to shove it against the glass wall. His forearm caught at the edge of the opening and twisted at an odd angle. She felt the crack of his bone before she heard it.

A cry ripped through his vocal cords as she lunged through the opening and threw herself on top of him. The metal tray clattered on the floor somewhere close to her.

With her legs straddled either side of him, her hands locked around his neck. She forced the weight of her body against her elbows as she pushed down on the man's trachea. She locked eyes with him as he choked. All he could do was squirm under her hold.

There was a slight movement at the corner of her eye, and before she could react, something sharp was driven into the side of her stomach; cutting deep into her skin and meeting flesh. As he drove it in deeper, Madison's grip on him slackened. She was pushed away as a litany of obscenities left the man's mouth. She gripped the side of her stomach as she crawled away from him. The wound felt damp under her fingers.

"You," he panted, "never fail to surprise me." He rose to his feet, with a stained knife in the grasp of his uninjured hand. "That scum, Hedrick, preferred younger girls. Misha was only seventeen when she gave birth to Charles. I wonder if Charles also shares his tastes. I, however, prefer older ones that can put up a fight," he spat as he lunged towards her.

Madison brought the tray up and slammed it as hard as she could square across his temple the moment he was within reach. The tray was heavy and thick. With the fourth hard strike to his head, he had gone limp.

She climbed up against the outer glass wall and felt blood trickling down her leg and soaking through the fabric of her pants and shirt. She hauled his unconscious body by the hand and dragged him inside the chamber. He was a heavy man, and the effort tore at her wound. By the time she was done, the slobber of her tears and snot, mixed with her blood, covered her whole face.

She locked the door and limped her way towards the closet. She had an idea where Aron was being held. She had doubted the purpose of the strange room with the trapdoor on the floor during her previous visit, but now she was almost sure about its true purpose. She slid the doors open and grabbed a shirt from a nearby hanger. She tied it across her waist and hoped it would stop the bleeding.

When she reached the far end of the closet, she threw open the curtains to the small room. Through its tinted glass doors, she made out the figure of a person settled on the floor.

She looked for something heavy to break the glass with and found a bronze vase wedged between two shelves.

"Hey," she called out against the door. "Are you in there?"

The reply came a few moments later. "I'm here! Who are you?"

"Listen, get away from the door, as far as you can, okay?"

"Okay!"

She gave him a final warning before slamming the vase against the tinted glass. A single crack formed on it at the impact, and she continued to slam it on that spot until the glass shattered to pieces.

Aron stood at a corner, studying her. "You're hurt," he said. Madison noticed the strap across his neck. It was linked to a chain that was nailed into the wall."

"Let's get out of here before he wakes up," she heaved, blinking away the dark spots in her eyes.

"I think there's an axe in there," he said, gesturing to the corner next to the door. A tall bag rested against it. "I tried to reach for it but couldn't."

At that, she noticed the marks around his neck. They bore an uncanny resemblance to the ones on Charles. She ran to the corner and carefully unzipped the bag. There was more than just an axe in there. At first glance she saw a crossbow and a machete.

"He said he used the crossbow to kill my mother," Aron whimpered. "He told me he'll do the same to the man who tried to help me."

"He won't hurt you now. Let's get you out of here," she said, grabbing for the axe. "Stand back."

When they made it out of the closet, she warily eyed the unconscious man lying inside the glass chamber. She wondered if he was dead but instantly pushed the thought away.

They raced out of the house and Madison was pleased to find that her car was still parked in the driveway. Uncharacter-istically, Madison had left her car unlocked and to her great relief the keys were still in the ignition.

"You're bleeding out," Aron commented as she drove to the Hampshire constabulary.

***

"Yeah. She got home an hour ago," Paul sighed. "She lost her phone. Okay, I'll do that."

Madison opened her eyes and the first thing that graced them was her ex-husband's frown.

"I know you're awake," he told her. "That was Allison. You didn't tell me you had me set as your emergency contact."

"Sorry," she muttered.

"She told me to tell you that the police arrived on time, and they got him. Who is she talking about? What happened to you?" he demanded as though he was at his wits' end. "You should be glad that wound wasn't too deep. But you've still lost a lot of blood."

The memory of Paul's horrified face as she stumbled in through the door flashed across her eyes. She felt guilty for getting him involved, but at that moment, it was either that or her inevitable death.

Madison felt for the wound at her side. "You patched me up?" she asked, as her fingers grazed the gauze wrapped around her stomach.

"I gave you first aid. But we still need to get you to a hospital," he insisted as he sat her up against the backrest of the couch.

"I will as soon as I can. Where is he?"

"Hasn't woken up yet. Now, tell me, where were you?"

"Out to find the Elwyn slayer," Madison answered. "He's been caught."

"What?"

21

"Mmm, listen to this," Paul started, turning to Madison as he read from the book. "'The blood-brain barrier is a lining of endothelial cells that keeps solutes circulating in adjoining blood vessels from entering the extracellular fluid of the CNS. So, it is basically an advanced security system of our body that keeps harmful things away from our big human brain. But in cases of Alzheimer's, the BBB prevents drugs that treat the disease from getting into the brain where it is essentially needed the most."

"In such cases, specifically engineered nanoparticles with the ability to cross over this barrier will carry and deliver the medicine to the affected parts of the brain.' This is from Antoine Andronico's journal," he said, shaking the small blue book at her. "He's the founder of Atomwise. Milkovich works for this guy."

"You think we should get him to one of the programs you mentioned?" she asked as she took the journal from him and skimmed through its pages.

"I think so. If things get out of hand, it could be worth a shot," Paul said as he stretched himself. "He is young enough; the treatment might work for him."

Madison nodded. After she had informed Paul about her findings, he was understandably furious that she had gone off alone.

But despite his animosity towards the situation, he refused to leave her side. They both knew how close to death she had come that day. That entire night she was restless and continuously shifted in bed. Paul was a heavy sleeper and thankfully did not stir.

When she woke up early the following day, she failed to notice the other man seated on the couch in their room; face in his palms. She yelped aloud when she finally did.

Charles looked up, startled, at her reaction. His eyes were swollen, and his face smeared with tears.

"What's wrong?" she asked as she slowly sat up. "Did it come back to you?"

"Yeah… you saved the kid, didn't you? That's why you're hurt."

"Yes. He's fine now."

"I'm glad," he expressed.

"You don't remember who attacked you, do you?"

"No. I remember nothing. I think my mind is blocking it out. But there was more than one person."

Madison's eyes widened. *That can't be.*

"Elizabeth?" she asked.

Charles nodded.

"I'm also guessing you already know who I am," she said.

Charles smiled, and she realised she had missed that look on him. "I do," he confessed. "I had initially planned on paying you off, but I genuinely enjoyed the time we shared together. I shouldn't have risked it, though; I was already losing it at that point."

"Glasgow furnishings is your account, isn't it? The one you used to withdraw the thirty million from your main account. And you did it during a very conveniently-timed system glitch.

How'd you accomplish all that?"

"I have connections. People who owe their lives to me, well, at least they think they do. All I needed was a ten-minute window, but I got five."

"Why did you do it?"

"Because I had a hunch as to why Elizabeth came back."

"What about the painting?"

"I don't know where it is. I'll be glad if it's gone. It was nothing but a reminder of my family's treachery. She can have the money as well. It's of more use to her than me."

"Then, what was the point of going through all this?"

"I wanted to live. I wanted to stand my ground and beat the curse, claim what's mine and keep it. I deserve that much, at least, after being abandoned by my own siblings. But it turns out that it was inevitable all along."

"You don't know that for sure."

"But I do! I have three years, four at best. There's no hope left for me."

"There's an organisation called Atomwise that can help you get better."

Just then, Paul's phone rang. It was loud enough to garner an aggravated curse from Paul. He handed Madison the phone. "I have to get this," she said excusing herself from the room.

"Hey, listen. I spoke with the broker," Allison said. "Elizabeth's in New York, at Simon Kane's current residence."

"What?" Madison yelled.

"She is registered under the name of Martha Herald under USCIS. And Martha Herald is Simon Kane's wife. They got married five years ago."

Madison's breath caught at those words.

"Look, I'll explain the rest later. I got Richards to trace her calls. And in the last two days, Martha Herald has been in contact with two men named John Peters and Thomas Drudge. These are aliases. They're bloody hitmen! And we traced their license plate, and they're here in Westminster. I think Charles is with them."

"No. He's with us," Madison announced. She realised she hadn't had the chance to tell her about Charles.

"What? Why? If he's with you, then they're coming for you!"

"Oh god," Madison breathed out.

"Go somewhere where they won't find you. Be careful, Madison," Allison gasped, before cutting the line.

If Elizabeth had indeed conspired with Henry, there was a good chance that she already had their home addresses. If her goons were looking for Charles, Madison's place would be the first on their checklist.

"We need to leave," Madison informed the two men as she rushed inside the room to pull out the duffel bag from underneath her bed.

"What, Where? What's wrong?" Paul asked as he scrambled out of bed.

"We need to get out of here. Elizabeth Fincher ordered a hit on her husband, and they could be here any moment."

Paul shot to his feet. "You're getting us into all kinds of trouble, Charlie," he informed. She could hear him explain the situation to Charles as she felt for her gun under the clothes in the bag.

Just as they reached Paul's car, a black SUV pulled up on the street across from the apartment complexes.

"Get in! Get in!" Paul yelled as he jumped into the driver's seat. Madison got in the back with Charles. She pushed him down until they were both crouched on the floor of the car.

Madison caught sight of Paul lighting a cigarette from the

corner of her eye. The sound of footsteps against weather-beaten gravel grew steadily louder as she realised that the men were making their way towards them.

"Hey, man!" a voice sounded from a distance. "Ya know a Madison Sharpe round here?"

"Uh, Nope. Don't know her," Paul responded. "Why? What's wrong?"

"None of your business, pal," the voice suggested as the sound of footsteps gradually receded from the car.

Paul fired the engine, and they headed off.

"Those are some huge suitcases they're carrying," Paul remarked on their way towards his house. "Wonder what's in there."

Madison grimaced at that and pulled herself on the seat. Charles begrudgingly followed suit. He looked shaken but remained quiet. She wondered if he was having one of his memory lapses again.

"Where to?" Paul asked.

"Somewhere public," she replied. "We can maybe head to your home later tonight."

They drove around most of the day and found a small diner near Mayfair where they had their lunch and where they remained till the evening. They finally left for Paul's house after having an early dinner.

Madison heaved a sigh of relief to find that his house was in one piece and not vandalised in any way.

"Okay. What do we do now?" Paul asked as he settled into the easy chair in his living room. Charles was fast asleep in one of the other rooms.

"We can't stay here for long."

"We'll leave in the morning then," he said as he leaned closer to her. "Why is his wife after him?"

"I have a few guesses, but… none of them would make sense to you."

"Try me."

Madison hesitated. "H-his wife hired me to look for a sum of money that had gone missing from his account. That money was the last bit of Charles' wealth, and she got together with him because of it. I think she knew that he was sick or would get ill eventually, and she could reap the benefits in the event of his death."

"And then there's her other husband, who's claiming that Charles had taken a loan from him. I think he was only there to rush the whole process."

"So, the whole money fiasco was to basically rob him of the money. Use you to get details about all his covert bank accounts, and now that she has all of it, she wants to get rid of him," Paul said, rubbing a finger at the tip of his nose.

"Exactly! It's all my fault."

"You're putting your life on the line for that man. I don't think you have much to be blamed for at the moment."

"So, what do you suggest we do?"

"He'll get killed here by himself, and when they eventually find us, we'll get killed along with him. We can either go to the police or… well, Atomwise operates in New Jersey. That's where we took Riley. We could leave at first light."

"It's worth a try. He's a helpless man," she said as she adjusted her clothing so it didn't rub against her wound.

"Is he just that, though?" Paul drawled, with an almost sad smile.

"What?" The sudden question caught Madison off guard, and she wondered if she had even heard it correctly.

"Nothing," he said, heaving a tired sigh. "I'll make some calls, arrange a meeting with the company. You get some sleep while we're still alive," he suggested as he got up from his chair and sauntered over to his room.

Madison leaned over as her gut clenched yet again with a pang of almost overbearing guilt.

As she closed her eyes, feeling the grip of sleep finally get to her, she wondered if she would dream of Livi again.

22

"Well, as much as I hate to say this, the decline is rapid in Mr Fincher's case. You told me he's been receiving treatment, is that correct?"

"Yes, he was, until recently." Madison nodded.

"Mr Fincher assured us that he wasn't on any antidepressants. The tests, however, say otherwise," Tyrone Milkovich asserted with a frown.

"What do you mean?"

"We've found large amounts of Amitriptyline in his blood. Which kind of comes as a shock to me since it is widely advised against in patients with dementia and other degenerative diseases," Tyrone drawled uneasily.

"Do you think someone fed it to him deliberately?" Paul asked the man.

"That is a possibility," Tyrone said, lightly nodding to himself. "I think it would be best if he stayed in our facility until we can guarantee his recovery."

Madison hesitated, but Paul nodded readily.

"Let me guide you through the procedures that we will undertake. Mr Fincher has already been made aware of them, but there is a high chance he might forget the important information. I need you to explain them to him again and get him to sign these," Tyrone pushed a set of papers towards them. "Willfully."

They were shown a small presentation on one of the larger LED screens in the room.

It was pretty much what Paul had been talking about a few nights before. Delicate matter, one to one hundred nanometers in size, which again is one-billionth of a meter, will be deployed into the hippocampus with the help of a specialised syringe, and the particles will traverse through the blood vessels and bypass the brain barrier to deliver the drugs to affected areas of the brain.

"Like an ultrafine delivery system, but instead of pizzas, these wee little engineered deliverymen would be delivering standard drugs used to treat Alzheimer's to the brain. It is not nearly as easy as it sounds, but all we can do is hope for the best."

"What's the worst that can happen?" Madison quizzed.

"It could trigger an aneurism, allergic reactions, or even a cerebral stroke. However, some of the world's finest surgeons will be present in the room at the time of the procedures," Tyrone replied. "He's in good hands, Miss Sharpe, I can assure you that much. But I do suggest you explain everything to Mr Fincher again and not leave anything out," Tyrone offered with a smile.

While Madison nervously paced the hotel room, Paul explained all the procedures to Charles for the second time that evening.

"I'll do it," Charles announced after Paul was done.

"But what if something goes wrong?" Madison argued.

"Well, that is a risk that I'm willing to take," Charles asserted, as he reached a hand out expectantly.

"Hand the man a pen, Maddie," Paul grumbled from where he stood.

"If something does go wrong, at least I'd die knowing that I'd tried. That it happened on my own terms. This is my decision to take Anne, I mean Madison."

"Here you go, buddy," Paul said as he passed a pen to the other man.

He walked over to Madison and gently squeezed her shoulder, "Let him do what he wants. It's late, go get some sleep. We have to leave early tomorrow to see him off."

Her eyes lingered on the other man. The lines around his neck were still prominent, but she knew they would heal eventually, as would the stab wound on his waist. If everything went as planned, he would soon return to the person he once used to be.

When she woke up in unfamiliar surroundings, it was still dark outside. Paul lay fast asleep next to her. She smiled at him and pressed a kiss against his brow before rolling out of bed. The one next to theirs was still untouched. Given Charles' recurrent loss of memory, they had collectively decided that staying together would be the best option.

She peered down the narrow hallway leading to the small living room. Charles was sitting on the couch, staring at the staticky telecast on the small TV that came with the room.

"Hey," she said as she tip-toed into the room.

"Hey," Charles said without turning.

"Are you feeling okay?" she asked, almost dreading the answer.

"I'm fine," he assured, as he finally faced her.

"Can't sleep?" she asked as she sat down next to him.

"No. I'm scared that if I fall asleep, I'll forget everything when I wake up again," he drawled with a sad smile.

She nodded at that.

"I saw a picture of you and Paul, back in Paul's house," he said as he returned his attention to the TV. "Was she your daughter?"

She knew that he was referring to the picture of herself, Paul and Livi, from their trip to Brighton. It was the only picture that Paul had refused to part with. Hence it still stood on the table near the entryway.

"Yes," she offered softly.

"What happened to her?" he asked, turning to face her again.

"She was killed three years ago," Madison admitted, looking down at her fingers. "I worked for the CID back then. I was pursuing a drug ring, and it was the first real case I had specifically asked to be assigned to after I had Livi. A month after I made my first arrest related to the case, the ring found out where I lived. They planted one of their men close to where we lived. He pretended to be a student and rented next door to us. There was no reason for me to suspect him. Paul and I often invited him over for dinner. But, one night, when Paul was away on a filming trip, and I was alone with Livi, the kid came in offering drinks like any other day. We cooked some Irish bread because he knew it was my favourite. But that night, he had slipped something in it. He and his men took Livi. They killed her. Left her body at…at a park just around the corner. The words: 'an eye for an eye' were spray painted on the grass next to her. She…she was only six. She had so much life ahead of her."

"I'm so sorry," Charles breathed out as he gaped at her.

"As expected, I was asked to step down from the case since I had a personal relationship with the victim. I was allowed to work again as long as I passed a mental health level, and stayed away from my daughter's case, which I did. When I was allowed back on the field I had this clarity, this desperation within me that wouldn't let me sleep or even breathe at times. I hunted their whole ring down like dogs and made sure that they rotted in jail for the rest of their lives."

"A little while later, when they received the maximum sentence, I quit my job, left Paul to drown in his misery while I drowned in mine, and that was that."

"You know it wasn't your fault," he said softly. His eyes were red and brimming with tears.

But it was.

"I know," she answered instead. "Would you like to tell me about the painting?"

"I thought you already knew all about it."

"I think I do. But it doesn't explain your uncle's devotion to it, or yours."

Charles wiped his face as he leaned back. "Well, this may take a while. My grandfather met my grandmother, Hirama, during the Blitz. She was an orphan who lived in Bristol and worked as a teacher.

"Amos ruined her life when he met her. He returned to Germany before the Blitz ended, and she had to deal with a pregnancy that was forced upon her. She gave birth to twins and raised them until he fled back to London and forced himself into their lives again. And along with him, he brought a painting."

"He hid it in my grandmother's home and hoped to make a fortune out of it. But he couldn't, amidst the chaos that followed the war; if he tried to sell it, then he'd have risked capture. So, he waited. But the right time never did come."

"He taught his children, or rather beat into them, the value of the painting as a world treasure and that their great father was able to capture it for them. He transferred his obsession with it to his impressionable children. He was a horrible man who did unspeakable things to his own kin."

"Eventually, their adulthood brought them freedom from their father. My uncle's talent, paired with my mother's beauty and intellect, brought them wealth and fame. But when Amos died, instead of surrendering the painting over to the government, my uncle locked it up in a trunk at his home and willed himself to forget about it. It was, after all, a reminder of the constant abuse he had faced at the hands of his own father, but he still couldn't bring himself to part with it."

"It was only after my mother passed away that I saw him take it out of the trunk and have it professionally restored. He set it up in my mother's room and spent countless nights just staring at it. It was his own personal hell, I supposed. One that he had to indulge in or risk losing all his sense of self. He passed it on to me because he was unable to part with it, even in death."

"Perhaps, my illness would've been of better use to him than me," Charles said with a humourless chuckle. "A merciful escape instead of a cruel existence."

Madison wouldn't have wished what Charles was going through on her worst enemy, but she somehow understood why he'd said that, and even found herself agreeing with him.

23

Paul and Madison walked Charles to the facility where Milkovich and Adrenico awaited him. Charles bade them goodbye and went on his way. Something about the way he behaved made Madison feel that a part of his memory had already dimmed away.

It was a four-month procedure, and their limited associations with Fincher didn't require them to stay in the country. Which was why Paul and Madison had returned home a week later after Tyrone promised that he would keep them informed about Charles' wellbeing.

After Henry's capture, he confessed to the abduction and murder of Sara Abbas as well as the murders of the many Fincher siblings. He directed the police to an underground chamber that the room in Charles' closet led to. There, they found the skeletal remains of the last two Fincher brothers, tied to metal chairs with their skulls severely fractured.

"And thus, the incense sticks?" Madison asked. "To hide the smell?"

"Exactly," Tudor answered. "But I still can't figure out what his motive was for killing Sara."

Madison had an uneasy feeling about that. She had been

receiving letters every week from Henry, asking her to meet with him since he was put on trial. What for, he didn't say. But she had a few guesses.

"Also, thank you for letting me take credit for this." Tudor added.

"You're not taking credit for anything. You found him, and you got him to speak. That's all that matters. And I should thank you for not bringing Charles in."

"We saved a lot of time by not bringing him in. Palmer was being unreasonable, but she gets it now. How is he, by the way? It's been a month, hasn't it?"

"Yeah, he's fine. He's healthy and doing well."

"Well, keep me updated."

"I will."

She had yet to tell Tudor about Henry's repeated requests for a meeting. In truth, she hadn't told anyone about it. Paul had found out when he saw the letters since she had the post office send all her mail to Paul's address for a little while. It surprised Madison that he didn't remark on them, despite how visibly furious he had been at the sight of the letters.

The two of them had stayed together for a few days after their return from New Jersey. But when no hitmen showed up at their door, after a whole week, she decided to move back to her apartment. Paul had initially disapproved of the idea, but he eventually gave in.

Elizabeth didn't contact her again, and Madison didn't expect her to do so anytime soon. If Charles decided to take Elizabeth to court, Madison would be more than willing to testify against her or help Charles make a solid case against her. But she doubted he would ever involve her in his affairs again or even remember her existence, for that matter.

More time had passed, and soon it was March. Due to the constant bad weather, riding classes at Elwyn were cancelled. Since she didn't have that many cases to work on, Madison had a lot of free time and could visit Karl and May more often.

"We're planning a trip to Thailand," May said as they sat at the table after supper, watching the two men at the sink washing dishes.

"I'll work for free next week if you can get him to stop teaching me a language that he himself doesn't understand, May," Phil offered.

"Shut your trap, boy," Karl grumbled as he slammed a hand against the younger man's back, causing the latter to holler in pain.

"Stop it, you two," May growled. "So, I was wondering if you would like to stay here while we're away. There's an empty room waiting just for you."

"May, not this again," Madison groaned.

"Listen to me, child. You don't have to move in if you don't want to, but the room's yours. All I'm saying is a change of scenery, being amidst nature," she said, spreading her arms out, "is good for the mind. And I know you love this place as much as we do."

"I have work, May."

"She wants you to quit," Karl said.

"I never said that," she spat at Karl. "I just said it would be good for you if you do. You could work at the farm with Phil. We'll even pay you a good wage, even more than Philly boy."

"May!" Phil objected. "I'm standing right here you know. Wait. She's actually considering it!" he exclaimed, pointing at Madison.

"Listen, love, take your time. I know it's a big decision, but I need you to know that there's no pressure on you whatsoever," May said, as she reached out and gently squeezed Madison's shoulder.

"Are you really going to live here?" Phil asked as he walked her to her car.

"Oh, I don't know."

"Well, think about it, okay? I'd love to have a partner. A strictly work one," he added quickly. "But you need to be ready to get your hands dirty if you're planning on working with me."

"Says the man who cried after seeing a body," she mocked.

"Hey! That was my first time ever seeing one in that condition."

"Well, death does that to you. You're fine now, though, right?" she asked, looking up at him.

"Yeah. I just had a bit of an existential crisis back then, but I'm all good now," Phil insisted.

"If you say so," Madison said as she got in her car. "But if you need anyone to talk to, I'm here for you."

"I know," he said with a grin as she turned on the ignition.

***

Madison was just about to get into bed when she received a text from Tyrone telling her that Charles was set to be released the following day.

She heaved a sigh at the news and dropped the phone back on the dresser. As she lay awake staring at the ceiling the thudding in her chest grew more intense.

She wanted to see him, to hear his voice, to have him smile at her again, but she wasn't sure if he wanted the same. Charles hadn't been in contact with her since they dropped him off at Atomwise, four months before, and she wasn't sure that he would when he was out.

If he didn't, she would move on from him. Hopefully, for good this time.

***

That morning, she pulled her hair into a bun, took a sip of her coffee and finished off her piece of toast before making her way to the car. She set the destination on her GPS to HMP Belmarsh, heaved a sigh, and then took off.

"You look incredible, Madison," Henry remarked.

"What do you want?" she said into the phone's mouthpiece, while glaring at the man seated in front of her; this time he was on the caged side of the glass.

"C'mon now. Would it hurt you to be a bit more pleasant?"

"Yes. It would."

"My lawyer tried to make me plead insanity, so I fired him. I felt really disrespected when he suggested that. And even if I did plead insanity, I'd end up in a mental hospital. That's far worse than a prison."

"Get to the point, Henry."

"I need you to give something to my cousin."

"What?"

"I'll tell you soon enough. But first, I'd like to tell you why I did what I did to Sara. Before everyone else in the courtroom hears about it tomorrow."

Madison braced herself as she eyed the man's sneer.

"I wanted Sara to create something for me. A perfect replica of Charles' painting. She was good at that sort of thing, and I would've let her go if she had behaved well. But by the time she was done perfecting her art, she was physically broken. There was no saving her, so I merely put her out of her misery. The one Elizabeth sent to Kane was that replica."

Madison's eyes brimmed with tears as she listened to the man. "Why? Why did she have to perfect the damn thing? Elizabeth wouldn't have known the difference."

"Elizabeth wouldn't, but Kane would. Thinking back, I'm not sure why I exerted her to the extent I did."

"I think I know why," Madison answered. "You wanted to see how far she could go, didn't you?"

A smile slipped on his lips. "And she went far and high to prove how perfect her art was. It was all worth it in the end."

"I hope you rot in there, Henry."

"I had it sent to your house," Henry said. "Tell Charles I miss him."

"You gave him away to Elizabeth's goons!"

"I also saved him from them and sent him to you so that you'd keep him safe. Which you did," Henry said. "So, well done, Madison."

***

When she finally found the guts to unwrap the frame-bound painting, she let out a little gasp.

She was finally looking at it - in person. The painting that had so many bad memories associated with it inspired so much hate within the people around it. And yet, oddly enough, when she looked at it she felt calm; the way she had when she saw Monet's works.

The scene was a familiar one, as were the colours used to depict it. She had seen it before in the glass chamber, on the piles and piles of canvases drawn by a luckless woman. And only then did she feel the hate rise in her. That's right. She loathed this painting.

She could destroy it. Pour some bleach on it or even burn it.

"Priceless evidence of humanity's success," she muttered to herself and almost guffawed.

Now she knew exactly what to do with it.

A few weeks later, Charles showed up at her place unannounced. His hair was longer, and he seemed to have put on some weight, which looked great on him.

"How have you been feeling?" she asked.

They were seated across from each other at Madison's dinner table. Somehow, she didn't feel as awkward with him as she had expected to feel.

"They cured me completely, can you believe it? I'm the first person to be successfully cured."

She knew that, of course. It had been all over the news. 'Charles Fincher, UK's multimillionaire entrepreneur, is the first man to have successfully beaten Alzheimer's,' the headlines had read.

Madison nodded with a fond smile. "You're the face of Atomwise."

"And you know this is all because of you," he said. "Thank you so much. And I don't think a sorry would do it, after everything you've been through."

She pursed her lips at that. "Did you speak to Elizabeth?"

"Yes. She couldn't get the money out. She tried to prove that it had been unlawfully transferred to the Glasgow account, but she had no evidence to back that claim since there was no record of the transfer ever taking place."

"And she was so sure that she had it all and that she wouldn't need me anymore. She even went ahead and ordered a hit on me. I don't understand how she thought any of this would work out."

"She can't sue the bank to have them compensate for the missing money because the original account belongs to me. And I am an able-bodied man who's also recently, very sound of mind. I am perfectly able to decide for myself, and I have decided that I will not be taking any action."

Madison clapped her hands as she let out a squeal of delight. "That is perfect. I'm so happy for you!"

Charles was momentarily taken aback by her reaction, but he broke into a grin. "Well, you seem happier."

"I must admit, I feel less burdened these days. I'm finally off my sleep meds as well. I can actually sleep without them."

Charles chuckled. "I'm glad I'm not the only one feeling invincible these days."

"Saying that would be a bit of a stretch for me. What happened to the painting?"

"Kane can keep it. I heard he sold it to an art collector."

"Do you know who they are?"

"The art collector? No, I'd rather not know. Tell me about you? What have *you* been up to?"

"Nothing much. I go about my day, have my food, and then wait around for you to call, which you never do."

All traces of humour and joy abandoned his face at those words. He opened his mouth as if to say something, but no words left him, as his eyes locked on to hers.

"How's Paul?" he asked.

"I let him go," she answered. "I think I would've just ended up holding him back if he had stayed with me. I think we both need a lot more time apart, even to consider starting something."

"Well, I respect that. He is a good man," he asserted with a fond smile. "But do let me drop by sometimes. I would like to be a part of your life if that's okay with you." He seemed hesitant and nervous, as if he had expected to be rejected from the very start, but after her confession something had changed in his eyes. And she realised that she quite liked that change.

"That would be nice."

***

"This is Allison, my subordinate," Madison informed Lukas.

"Hello, I'm Lukas," he said, shaking her subordinate's hand. "Are you ready to see a miracle, Allison?"

Allison looked quizzically at the men and then back at Madison. "Sure, I suppose," she replied.

Lukas led them into a vast storage room and through tables and shelves filled with art pieces that were not on display at the gallery.

She spotted the painting spread out on one of the many tables.

"This is it," Lukas declared as they reached the table. "This belongs to the Water Lilies series by Monet. A truly priceless find, Madison."

"It's pretty," Allison remarked. "But I still can't believe a woman got killed over this."

Madison agreed with that sentiment of hers.

"People are kind of awful," Allison declared with a frown.

Madison found herself agreeing to that as well.

"Will they put it on display?" Madison asked.

"No. It's Nazi-looted art. People won't react well to it."

"So, you'll just keep it locked away forever?" Allison asked.

"Of course not! Some people will be allowed to access it for research purposes, it might even be displayed publicly during some exhibitions, but that's about it."

"That's truly a pity," Allison remarked. "It's quite nice to look at."

***

"Anne Shirley? Is that you?" Phil inquired as he brushed down a brown colt by the gates to the barn. "Oh, wait, what? Am I seeing things?" he remarked, rubbing a hand mockingly on his eyes. "Good god, did the sun rise from the west this morn? Oh, are you really wearing a helmet?"

"As a matter of fact I am, sire," Madison expressed, tipping her hat at the other man as she led her horse, Emily, towards him.

"A genuine reply? The world must be ending," he proclaimed dramatically.

"Oh, shut up!" She got down from the saddle and handed him the reins to the horse.

"I feel good lately," she announced humorously as she watched him tie down the reins to one of the posts. "I feel like I've changed a lot. In a good way," she added as she leaned effortlessly against the fence.

"Well, life is all about changes. But if the change is a positive one, it is truly a victorious feat," he offered smartly.

"Indeed," she muttered as she tipped her head back and closed her eyes, feeling the gentle brush of the wet breeze against her skin. "I've been thinking, maybe I should take May up on that offer. Will you teach me the work around here, sire?"

"Really?" Phil gasped. "Oh well, if that's the case, I'll be more than happy to."

Printed in Great Britain
by Amazon